Which Big Giver Stole the Chopped Liver?

Also by Sharon Kahn
in Large Print:

Hold the Cream Cheese, Kill the Lox
Don't Cry for Me, Hot Pastrami

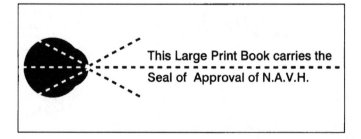

Which Big Giver Stole the Chopped Liver?

A Ruby, the Rabbi's Wife Mystery

Sharon Kahn

Thorndike Press • Waterville, Maine

Published in 2004 by arrangement with Scribner, an imprint of Simon & Schuster, Inc.

Thorndike Press® Large Print Core.

The tree indicium is a trademark of Thorndike Press.

The text of this Large Print edition is unabridged. Other aspects of the book may vary from the original edition.

Set in 16 pt. Plantin by Myrna S. Raven.

Printed in the United States on permanent paper.

Library of Congress Cataloging-in-Publication Data

Kahn, Sharon, 1934–
    Which big giver stole the chopped liver? : a Ruby, the rabbi's wife mystery / Sharon Kahn.
        p. cm.
    ISBN 0-7862-7024-1 (lg. print : hc : alk. paper)
    1. Rothman, Ruby (Fictitious character) — Fiction.
2. Rich people — Crimes against — Fiction.   3. Women detectives — Texas — Fiction.   4. Rabbis' spouses — Fiction.   5. Jewish women — Fiction.   6. Texas — Fiction.
7. Large type books.   I. Title.
PS3561.A397W48 2004b
    813′.54—dc22   2004054901

To a future **Ruby** *reader*
— *my dearest Emma* —
on the occasion of her Bat Mitzvah

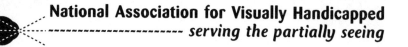

National Association for Visually Handicapped
-------------------- *serving the partially seeing*

As the Founder/CEO of NAVH, the only national health agency solely devoted to those who, although not totally blind, have an eye disease which could lead to serious visual impairment, I am pleased to recognize Thorndike Press* as one of the leading publishers in the large print field.

Founded in 1954 in San Francisco to prepare large print textbooks for partially seeing children, NAVH became the pioneer and standard setting agency in the preparation of large type.

Today, those publishers who meet our standards carry the prestigious "Seal of Approval" indicating high quality large print. We are delighted that Thorndike Press is one of the publishers whose titles meet these standards. We are also pleased to recognize the significant contribution Thorndike Press is making in this important and growing field.

Lorraine H. Marchi, L.H.D.
Founder/CEO
NAVH

* Thorndike Press encompasses the following imprints: Thorndike, Wheeler, Walker and Large Pr int Press.

1

"What do you think, Ruby?"

"I'm thinking pimento cheese and tuna fish disguised as a sushi roll doesn't do it for me, Essie Sue."

I use my cocktail napkin to remove all traces of the inedible faux sushi she's just forced through my lips with her Verry Berry talons.

"But the chef says he'll name it the Essie Sue Roll in honor of our booking the hotel party rooms."

"Maybe that should tell you something about how desperate he is for business." Milt Aboud's low growl is barely audible in the background, but Essie Sue hears it.

"He's not desperate at all — you know this hotel is the best convention site in Austin. In fact, I had to talk the manager into squeezing our Temple Rita reunion group into the hotel at the same time they're hosting a world-famous convention. This is the final menu-tasting session — the others didn't go well."

Essie Sue doesn't miss the look Milt gives me.

"You're just jealous, Milt, because you and Ruby aren't getting this banquet catering job for The Hot Bagel. You're already catering the closing Donor Breakfast at the temple — what more do you want?"

"Oh, we're desperate, too," Milt says, "sales have been down all year. And you can bet your Lexus I wouldn't have driven all the way up from Eternal to Austin for reasons other than financial."

Milt's my working partner in our bakery, The Hot Bagel, and not exactly a fan of Essie Sue's, although in emergencies, I notice she always wants his opinion. Not that she listens. She's been asking and not taking my own advice for years, ever since my late husband Stu came to Eternal as rabbi of Temple Rita. Yes, Rita. Essie Sue was head of the Rabbinical Selection Committee at the time, and in a masterful stroke of self-perpetuation, engineered her own election as Permanent Chair of the Temple Board a few years ago.

The three of us, Milt, Essie Sue, and I are sitting at a lone folding table under a huge crystal chandelier, sampling food served by what looks like the entire hotel catering staff. Essie Sue's bites are always minuscule, in pursuit of perpetual thinness, which she's already attained six times over. Her Tawny Blonde page boy of years past — way past — has flipped outward and upward this year in the latest svelte cut, but still remains as tawny and moussed as ever.

This room could easily hold several hundred people, which is one reason I'm wondering why our event, planned for a mere fraction of that number, is being given such attention. Maybe the hotel is desperate, but the more obvious answer is that the banquet manager, like the rest of us, succumbed to Essie Sue's Godfather treatment.

"I told them cheap but elegant," Essie Sue informs us as we're served something called Imitation Caviar, which more than proves the point, with the emphasis on cheap. Milt shifts in his chair in an effort to escape, but before he can get up, an assistant hotel manager makes an appearance.

"I've brought along my own caterer from Eternal," Essie Sue tells the manager, "and he's quite taken with your spread."

"Yeah, taken ill," Milt says in my ear, and I kick him to behave. We honestly can't afford not to get at least part of this reunion for The Hot Bagel. What my interest in our partnership earns isn't enough to support me, and it's rough going even with my second job as a computer consultant.

Fortunately, the manager doesn't notice my boot under the table. He's more interested in the bookings.

"What's your latest count on the hotel guests? And it's for what special occasion, Mrs. Margolis . . . ?"

Essie Sue sticks an engraved invitation in his face by way of explanation, though in my opinion, it looks more like a summons to a séance than to a reunion:

Come One, Come Some
You Are Cordially Invited to

La Dolce Vita Temple Rita —
Homecoming for the Long-Gone

Join This Exciting Reunion of Those
Who Have Departed from Our Beloved
Eternal, Texas, and Have Gone on
to Greener Pastures
(Psalm 23: He maketh me to lie down
in green pastures . . .)

What Have You Made of Yourself?
Share Your Lives, and Especially
Your Bounty with the Congregation

That Shaped What You Are Today.
Our Founding Fenstermeister Family
Will Be Honored Along with the Lifetime
Chairwoman of the Board,
Mrs. Essie Sue Margolis.
Major Donor Reception Planned
for the More Fortunate.

(Dates, places, and events
on enclosed sheet)

"So this is a reunion of your temple in Eternal?"

"Odd, isn't it," I say, unable to resist pointing out one more time that the idea of having a small-town congregational re-union at a fancy Austin hotel is beyond ludicrous.

"Don't pay any attention to Ruby," Essie Sue says. "She has no imagination. As a manager of a sophisticated establishment, you'll have no trouble understanding that if one wants to attract the affluent, one must give them an elegant setting. Why offer them accommodations in Eternal when they can go four-star in Austin?"

"Maybe because they're supposed to be reuniting in their own hometown?" Milt does get to his feet this time.

"What's all this with the affluent?" I ask.

"How about the great unwashed, like most of us at Temple Rita? It's our reunion, too."

"You weren't even confirmed at Temple, Ruby — the reunion's really not for you. You're embarrassing the manager."

I leap up from the chair myself this time, but not before the assistant manager, who knows a getaway line when he hears one, starts making his excuses.

"So before you go," Milt asks him, "you say your hotel is booked for the same time with another gathering?"

"Fully booked. With overflow. Ordinarily, you wouldn't have a chance this week. Unfortunately, Mrs. Margolis produced a reservation for your group made three years ago and confirmed in the previous manager's files."

"You made this reservation three years ago, Essie Sue?" I ask.

"Right after that mini reunion of my confirmation class," she says. "I figured we might want to expand the reunion next time and make a fund-raiser out of it, and that's exactly what developed."

Aside from the fact that she makes a fund-raiser out of everything, she's nothing if not persistent.

"I told Mrs. Margolis we'd give her a much better deal if she'd change the date, and your group would find a quiet weekend to be more enjoyable," the manager says, "but she wants this one — less than a week from today."

Naturally.

"And what's the group that's booked with ours?" I ask.

"It's KillerCon, an international mystery convention."

I'm excited. Maybe Josie Joaquin's here.

"I have a friend from high school who's a mystery writer," I say, "and a well-known one. She may be here."

"Well, we have over fifteen hundred registrants. We're quite honored that they chose Austin and our hotel in the heart of downtown — it shows what important projects we can take on these days. Truly amazing."

The man has no idea.

2

Here's the invitation to the event you boycotted — I scanned it for you so you could see what I have to look forward to this week. Have you ever heard of such a *long* reunion? They'll be sick of one another all the way from Wednesday night arrival through Monday's final breakfast. Essie Sue's convinced that the longer they stay, the more donations she can pry out of them.

Aren't you sorry now that you asked me to leave you off the list? Your grad school years as a temple member more than qualify you, in case you change your mind. Not to mention your status as my best friend! Now that you're making real lawyer money for the plane fare, you could use the reunion as an excuse to come stay with me. Maybe I'll sleep better if you're here — I've had a devil of a time sleeping through the night lately — to the point where my doctor's referred me to a sleep apnea specialist.

E-mail from: Nan
To: Ruby
Subject: *One of My Wiser Decisions*

No thanks — I'm not changing my mind. You just want company in your misery, although I *am* sorry you're having sleep problems, too. But really, it would be a horrible time to try and have a visit. You'll be lucky if you get two minutes to yourself with Essie Sue conducting a bi-city extravaganza.

You didn't include the dates and events — are there gleanings scheduled for the *less* fortunate?

What Fenstermeisters are left standing after all these years? I haven't heard you mention them in ages.

E-mail from: Ruby
To: Nan
Subject: *Freddie Fenstermeister*

The Founding Son, Freddie — a former college linebacker — used to look more like a Foundling Son, but the trophy wife took him in hand and now he has that CEO-ish silver mane sculpted in granite. And the manicured nails and the gum implants. Okay, Freddie isn't a son — he's Miss Rita Fenstermeister's grand-nephew, the only family member alive today.

Miss Rita, as you know, was the one who inherited the family fortune, and who basically left the money to build the Temple on the condition it was to be named after her. Fortunately, someone came up with the brilliant idea of calling it Temple Rita instead of Temple Fenstermeister.

Freddie's grandfather, Miss Rita's brother, was the black sheep — or at the very least, gray. I don't know why he was in disfavor, but after Miss Rita's death and some protracted litigation, he inherited the family hat factory in 1930. I'm assuming there was lots of money in addition to the factory, because if Freddie has big bucks today, it certainly ain't from hats. And I can assure you he's more than well-off if Essie Sue's honoring him. He and she have always competed for the position of *who really runs the Temple* — Essie Sue wins in the public arena, but Freddie considers himself the founding power broker. Freddie and Essie Sue's husband Hal were college frat brothers, too, and there's been a rivalry there for years.

Unfortunately, Freddie also has a problem with Rabbi Kevin. I don't have time to go into it now, but he can't stand Kevin ever since Kevin insulted the Fenstermeisters by forgetting to read the names of their departed at last year's memorial service. Held at the Founders Circle of the temple cemetery, of all places. My Stu would have talked his way out of it, but Kevin, as you well know, never had the knack. I'm meeting him later, in fact, to help with his reunion welcoming speech. I'll keep you posted.

3

The rabbi's study still reminds me of a furniture store display. Kevin Kapstein has been in Eternal for one contract term already, and the place doesn't look lived in yet. I don't expect it to look like it did over five years ago when Stu was rabbi and the whole town would drop in to sit on the floor pillows or shlump all over the worn sofas. Essie Sue was probably right when she called for a renovation after Stu's death, even though I hated to see it at the time. Kevin deserved a new start. It's just that his choices (or hers) were so imposingly corporate. That credenza is as polished and untouched as the day they delivered it. And people don't drop in anymore — they make appointments. Like I did today, at Kevin's request.

Which is why I'm furious that I'm here and he isn't.

I'm about to leave a note and go over to The Hot Bagel to review accounts, when I hear a clatter in the hallway — unmistakably our rabbi with his arms too full. His paunch helps him hold up his bundles, but also contributes to his breathlessness.

Beads of sweat are perched at the edge of his receding hairline, and his white dress shirt doesn't look as if it's going to hold up past noon.

"Sorry, Ruby. I thought you'd be late, so I made a stop at the post office box — I rented a huge one for all my journals."

"Am I usually late, Kevin?" The man has this way of putting you on the defensive by turning his mistakes into yours, and I've been trapped by it more than I like to admit.

He ignores my remark, of course, and makes a point of fanning the biblical and rabbinic journals across the front of his desk, facing outward.

"Do you read all those?" I can't resist — the fanning outward makes me do it. "It's me, Kevin."

He looks up and gives me one of the few straight answers I've ever received from him.

"No, but sometimes I scan the introductions on the john."

We both burst out laughing, and I must say the encounter puts me in a much better mood for the morning's chore.

"Okay," I say, "let's dispense with the intellectual discussion and take a look at your reunion talk. Why do I have to critique this one? You write speeches all the time."

"Because I'm under a lot of pressure for this reunion. Essie Sue told me that I have to make a good showing in front of all these returning members — especially the ones she's targeting for big gifts. Now that Eternal's growing, she wants to use this event to enhance the Temple's image."

"Eternal's growing? By how much?"

"We got fifty new people in town last year, I think. Of course, none of them is Jewish."

"So Eternal's supposed growth is her motivation to improve the Temple? And you?"

"I guess so. I don't question her motivation, Ruby — I just stay out of her way. The founding family already hates me, so I need her on my side."

I wish it weren't so, but his take on Essie Sue is probably saving his job. Her competition with the Fenstermeisters is so fierce that any enemy of theirs is a friend of hers. Besides, she doesn't want a new rabbi who might challenge her unquestioned leadership, so she has a stake in keeping Kevin in place.

"I don't exactly get it," I say. "Who's pressuring you — Essie Sue or the Fenstermeisters?"

20

"Essie Sue was very blunt about it. She said if I didn't get with the program and show more excitement about this stellar re-union of all our members who've left town, I might be axed."

"What does she expect from this gala, aside from personal glorification and more contributions? I've tried to stay out of it and concentrate on the catering we're doing — such as it is — so I'm out of the loop."

"She wants to redo the temple sanc-tuary, and that takes big money."

Oy. The sanctuary's the one part of our building that has real charm and a sense of history.

"I'll admit the dark-paneled walls are a little gloomy," I say, "but the stained-glass windows illuminate the space — I think it works really well, don't you?"

"I like it, but Essie Sue's decided we need to come into the modern age. She's thinking all glass and steel — like the new actors' theater in Austin."

"Yikes . . . the one with the pipes all showing on the ceiling? I can just picture this. It'll be a miniature monstrosity."

"Not so miniature. She believes we should build bigger for the future even if our membership is staying the same."

"Say no more. I get the picture. Essie Sue will have to step over me if she wants steel pipes."

I read Kevin's welcoming speech, which is unexceptional, bordering on dull, but it doesn't insult anyone or otherwise get him in trouble, which I suppose was his primary goal.

"The only way I'd improve this if I were you is to throw in one graph each of glowing praise for Essie Sue and Freddie Fenstermeister."

"I thought of it, but I was afraid each one would feel that what I said about the other was better."

I can't argue with that — Kevin's obviously more tuned in to his predicament than I would have imagined. So we compromise and compose a sickeningly complimentary section about their joint devotion to Temple Rita, and I'm thankful the whole thing's only taken an hour out of my day, especially since tonight we're going to the hotel to welcome the reunion guests. Essie Sue's chartered a bus to bring the whole committee to the hotel and back after the event.

"By the way, Ruby, is your boyfriend coming up from San Antonio for the reunion?"

I pause on my way out the door.

"Not if he can help it." Kevin never calls Ed Levinger by his name, I notice. Despite the fact that our one arranged date was a disaster, Kevin still likes to believe that he and I *went* together. I assumed that was in the past tense, but you never know with Kevin.

"Are you two still tight, Ruby?"

"Well, if you have to ask, I guess I'll have to reevaluate whether we are or not. If you mean are we still going together, though, the answer is *yes*."

"I don't see him up here much."

"You know he travels a lot for the newspaper," I say as I'm out the door.

I can tolerate Kevin a lot better than I used to, and I'm even fond of him in a weird sort of way, but I draw the line at making him my confidant. On the other hand, when he's disarmingly frank like this, he does make me think.

I'm sitting in the temple parking lot in a funk over what he's brought up, actually. If I'm honest with myself, I'd have to say that Ed and I are more or less stalled. The intensity's still there when we're together, but it often goes negative, and neither of us is very good at making it better.

I'm frankly frustrated that I don't see

him more, and that when I do, it's unsatisfying. His job at the paper in San Antonio keeps him busy, but still. I've asked him to come up for the reunion banquet, but so far, he's balking. It's not that I think he'll have a good time — it's just that I want him to do this for me, since I'd do the same for him, and have. At this point, the only thing that will get him up fast is if he hears that I've invited police lieutenant Paul Lundy to take me, and I haven't stooped that low. Yet.

4

We file onto Essie Sue's bus tonight with all the enthusiasm of Bar Mitzvah kids writing thank-you notes. Most of us wanted to do the entertaining here at home — no schlepping, no fuss — but that's history. Although we only have a thirty-minute ride from Eternal to Austin, Essie Sue's organized the trip like a cross-country tour group, complete with singing on the bus (a silent failure), games (no takers), and a pep talk, which, since she's the only one involved, is proceeding apace.

"People, first and foremost I want you not to embarrass Temple Rita in any way during this reunion. This could spoil the mood of the prospective donors."

Unless it's my imagination, she's looking at me during this diatribe, but then, I'm paranoid when it comes to Essie Sue. Besides, she has other targets.

"My cochairman, Mr. Fred Fenstermeister, has unfortunately refused to travel with us in fellowship on the bus — he'll be driving up in his Mercedes.

"There are over a hundred registrants attending, and to please everyone, I've planned some of the activities in Austin and others in Eternal. Listen closely — this will be the order of events:

"Tonight — Wednesday, those of us on the welcoming committee will greet the guests informally at our banner-waving ceremony. Thursday we'll concentrate all our efforts on the very significant LOCO Cocktail Party (Large Outstanding Contributors Only) at the hotel at 7 p.m. Other guests will be provided for. Friday we journey down to Eternal in private cars and chartered buses for day tours of our town's new additions, followed by Shabbat services, and hospitality overnight. After enjoying the Shabbat in Eternal, Saturday evening we'll bus back to Austin to meet and greet and enjoy a traveling exhibit of Jewish ceremonial art, followed by our Grand Reunion Banquet on Sunday night. The final breakfast in Eternal, catered by The Hot Bagel, will take place on Monday, giving all of you an early start for home that day."

"Are you furnishing medications for motion sickness?" Buster Copeland, one of my more reliable allies, yells from the back of the bus.

"Isn't there any way you could have

avoided all these backs and forths?"

"My transportation committee agreed that the travel adds adventure to the reunion."

Her transportation committee consisted of herself, the manager of the charter company, and husband Hal, who settled for taxation without representation forty years ago as a means of survival.

I raise my hand.

"Yes, Ruby?"

"Can you elaborate on 'others will be provided for' Thursday night? I'd like to know what the peons will be doing while the big donors wine and dine."

"We've been over this, Ruby, and you understand — you just don't agree."

She's right — and that pretty much sums up our whole personal history. But at least I'm making her spell out how she's discriminating against anyone who's not a big donor.

"There's a perfectly delightful beer and pizza garden on the hotel mezzanine, and they're reserving a special section, Dutch treat, for those at our reunion who can't give their *all*. Those who can will be treated to champagne, assorted fancy nuts excluding peanuts, and a State of Texas chopped liver mold made with loving hands by yours truly. We will also feature sushi customized by the hotel chef, and other round-the-world hors d'oeuvres representing our ancestors' countries of origin."

"Who's Japanese?" Buster wants to know. He doesn't get an answer.

Having tasted some of the chef's offerings, pizza and beer don't sound half bad. I predict a grand rush to the mezzanine tomorrow night. I'm interested to hear, though, that Francie Fenstermeister, Freddie's wife, lost the battle of the chopped liver molds. She and Essie Sue both fancy themselves great cooks, and I'm sure Francie didn't give up easily. Essie Sue must have threatened her life.

Our bus disgorges us at the lobby entrance. Two paper streamers thrown together by the Temple Teens don't make it down the bus steps, while a cloth WELCOME TO ETERNAL banner carried reluctantly by the Spry Seniors survives long enough to get caught in the revolving door. Which is a good thing, since we're not *in* Eternal — we're in Austin, and our guests will be confused enough after hearing the schedule of events.

There's not a hotel employee in sight at the front entrance. As we walk into the lobby, I understand why. The hotel workers are busy getting ready for the big mystery convention, which begins to-morrow but is dwarfing us already, and we've been here all of five minutes. Commercial banners are going up on the balconies and people shouting directions are filling up the service elevators with folding tables.

When we finally summon someone to the reception desk, she informs us that our group is gathering on the Foundation Level. That's hotel-speak for the basement. Since the elevators and escalators have been preempted by preparations for KillerCon, we lug any surviving greeting material down the back stairs.

We're late, of course, and to add to the general chaos, Essie Sue has outsmarted herself. She's insisted that the hotel hold up the refreshments until she could give the word, and they've followed her orders. One hundred or so hungry, thirsty, and un-happy reunion participants have been stuffed into a space the size of my upstairs bedroom without so much as a glass of water. She's mobbed, but undaunted, and heads toward the microphone near the door.

"Welcome one and all. As soon as I notify the waiters, our reception will begin. Please line up to receive your name tags and goody bags."

"Forget the goody bags — just give us some ice water."

"How about a cold beer?"

"Hold on, ladies and gentlemen — you need to be properly welcomed to La Dolce Vita at Temple Rita."

"Why *aren't* we at Temple Rita?"

I'd like to see her explain that one, but she ignores it as she pushes the ten people closest to her into a makeshift line. The waiters appear with food and drink, and the line dissolves into the crush of bodies.

I recognize many old friends, and when I don't, I check my jacket pocket for a cheat sheet — the proof pages for the program book we've compiled, complete with photos. I've also left a message for my high school author friend at the mystery convention.

We're actually having fun, which obviously isn't part of the overall plan. Essie Sue is determined to form a line, even though the crowd is proving adept at finding name tags without further instruction.

"You need your goody bags, and I must have your name signed in the registration book, people."

They've picked up their own goody bags, too — it's only the registration book that's suffered.

Allison Levy, a reunion guest who's an ex-president of the temple Sisterhood and no stranger to Essie Sue's tactics, asks if I've had anything to do with the giveaways.

"Are you kidding?" I answer. "She wouldn't let me anywhere near them — her husband Hal's nieces filled the bags with her."

I take a look at Allison's bag, and believe me, the word *goody* is a stretch by any measure. First we pull out three free coupons to the Lube Rack of Eternal — that's appropriate, considering these people won't be here after this week. Essie Sue's splurged on half a dozen hard candies, a plastic pocket comb, a one-ounce box of raisins, a paper bookmark from our recent Humane Society banquet, and in a futile attempt at relevance, a calendar of Jewish holidays, which expires next month.

"No wonder she wouldn't let me near these," I say. I start to apologize, but Allison won't hear it. I guess as a former president of the Sisterhood, she needs no explanation.

"Who's that guy?" she asks.

I follow her eyes, then grab my cheat

sheet, but can't find him. There's something odd about the man she's pointing out, or quite a bit odd, I should say. He needs a shave, although he could be starting a beard — that's not such an easy call these days. His green plaid pants look as though he's just come off some golf course, and he's wearing them with a brand-new light green dress shirt and wrinkled paisley tie. His run-down black leather sneakers complete the outfit — a weird amalgam of old and new.

"Maybe he's some ex-member's husband," I say. It's obvious that neither one of us believes *that,* and I'm about to go over and introduce myself when I notice the crowd stirring in the direction of the door. All I can see is Freddie Fenstermeister's elegantly coiffed do, rising above the throng. Freddie is six foot two at least, and with his sleek head serving as a beacon, I'm able to move through the mob scene to see what's going on.

"This is it?" he says to me. "This is the space Essie Sue's reserved for over a hundred people?"

"Hi, Francie," I say to his peripatetic second wife, who's about to wander out of orbit to find a drink. She used to be the tolerable one in the family, despite what Essie Sue said about her. I liked having her on hand whenever I took on Freddie, but in the last few years she's become his clone.

"You'd better keep him away from the Margolises, Ruby," she says in passing. I grab her hand.

"Not so fast. I came over here to find out what's going on between Freddie and Essie Sue. Can't they stifle it during the reunion at least?"

"Why don't you ask me?" Freddie says. "The woman's not only bossy, she's incompetent, too. Nobody in her right mind would stuff so many people into this closet — not with all the money this is costing."

"I understand you're helping underwrite a lot of it," I say in my most conciliatory tone.

"More than her cheap husband Hal is doing. I understand he's in a lot of financial trouble, by the way."

My *stay-away-from-this* vibe is kicking in fast. I learned a long time ago not to hang around when someone like Freddie shares these not-so-innocent confidences.

I leave Freddie to his glad-handing — he's certainly taking this cochairing seriously. Within a five-minute span, I see him giving his hearty smile and handshake to a string of guests — Brother Copeland's in-laws from Little Rock, the guy in the green plaid pants, and one of our former temple treasurers, who's moved to Michigan.

Essie Sue's doing her share of politicking, too, on the other side of the room. I guess we can consider ourselves lucky that they're not going mano a mano.

"Freddie thinks he's a big shot because he's taken a suite upstairs," she tells me.

"I thought the whole place was sold out except our block of rooms," I say.

"Not his suite — it's the Presidential Penthouse Suite. He paid plenty for it."

"So what, Essie Sue? Why can't you relax and enjoy the reunion like everyone else? After all, you and Freddie aren't running for anything — you're cochairs."

"Where's the rabbi?" she asks. I'm used to having Essie Sue change the subject in mid-sentence, but it's still disconcerting. I point to a waiter who's apparently giving Kevin first dibs at a fresh plate of the faux sushi Essie Sue ordered. Only Kevin would have the nerve.

With one hand Essie Sue grabs my wrist, and with the other she grasps Kevin's elbow, steering us both toward a couple I don't know.

"Rabbi and Ruby, I want you to meet two of our most honored guests — Charles and Cynthia Stone. They've come all the way from California to attend the reunion, and we were all in confirmation class together when we were sixteen."

While I'm saying hello to this well-dressed couple, Essie Sue hisses to Kevin, "Plan A."

He's frozen in the headlights, which isn't unusual, and it dawns on me that Plan A is a code from the *How to Get Donations* workshop she conducted last week.

"What's Plan A?" Kevin whispers. Except that since he's never been able to master whispering, we all hear him. I do my bit to divert the Stones while Essie Sue and Kevin get their codes straight.

"It's so nice to have you here," I manage to say before Essie Sue interrupts.

"Rabbi," she says, ignoring me as usual, "ask Charles and Cynthia about the wonderful memories which bring them here."

"I'm refreshing his memory about Plan A," she hisses in my ear. "If you remind big givers of precious memories connected with the Temple, they'll contribute more. And a rabbi can do it better than other people."

Not this one, but if she doesn't know that by now, she's not hearing it from me.

"Uh, what *are* your memories?" Kevin asks them, looking at me to see how he did. I guess he doesn't dare glance at Essie Sue.

"What do I recall about confirmation, you mean?" Charles says. "I remember my kid brother sticking his leg into the aisle as I marched down to receive my blessing. I broke my ankle and couldn't play football for the next season.

"And I was the captain," he says, looking more pained by the second.

"Oh." Kevin looks at Essie Sue this time. "What was Plan B again?" he says.

"Family," she says in his ear.

"If all else fails, involve the family," she mouths to me. "People love their families."

"So what are your memories, Mrs. Stone?" Kevin says.

Mrs. Stone was obviously fortified before she came — the bargain zinfandel the waiters are pouring wouldn't affect a fly.

"At sixteen?" She gives out something between a snort and a sniffle. "At sixteen, I didn't have the sense to stay away from pimply-faced football captains. We had to get married the next year. Remember, Essie Sue?"

"So you started a little early," Essie Sue recovers. "You have a wonderful son from the experience. How is Justin, by the way?"

"Serving time for embezzlement," Charles says. "He embezzled from his own father's business."

The Stones' mood is heading south fast, but Essie Sue's undaunted.

"I'm sure the rabbi can counsel you while you're at the reunion — that's what he's here for," she says.

"I am?" Kevin looks heavenward but doesn't seem to be receiving anything inspiration-wise.

"So why are you here?" he finally blurts out.

"They're here to celebrate the good old days," Essie Sue says.

"I'll take care of the Stones," she leans over and says to me as she attempts to throw an arm around each of them. "Depending on how much was embezzled, they might only be suitable for Plan C. Alert the rabbi."

Kevin remembers Plan C — it figures. "Plan C is for *don't bother.*"

I'm just about to express my relief, when Kevin looks past me toward the door. When I turn around to see, too, I'm blown away.

"Hi, Mom." A tall, wiry redhead comes toward me with his arms open for a hug.

It's Joshie.

5

If he weren't holding me up, I'd have to sit down — my knees aren't functioning at all. For my son Josh, as with most single guys in their early twenties, home is definitely *not* where the heart is. It's where Mom is, though, and when he can't get me to come to him, he comes home to me.

"I thought I'd surprise you," he says, grinning, "even though I know you're going to remind me you hate surprises."

"I do, but not this one. Especially in the midst of Reunion Week — maybe now I can actually get through it. Don't tell me Essie Sue brought you in from North Carolina?" I look around for her, but she's off meeting and greeting.

"No, but I did get an invitation, and since you've been noodging me to get myself down here, I decided to grab a cheap online fare at the last minute. I brought you another surprise besides myself, but I left it at the house."

"You've already been home?"

"I have to admit Watermelon Lane looked pretty good to me. I didn't realize

I'd missed the place. And Oy Vey went nuts when she saw me from the backyard."

"She misses you something awful, Joshie. Unlike me, of course."

I hang on to him until we can find two chairs at the back of the room.

"You didn't bring someone with you, did you?"

"You mean a girlfriend? No, Mom. That's not the surprise. But I'm still seeing Claire more than anyone else — you met her on your last trip."

"I'm glad to get the update, but believe me, I'm not pushing for anything. That's the least of my worries."

"So what *are* your worries?"

"About you? None, really. Let's get out of here so we can catch up. Unless you want to see people. I'm being selfish as usual, and it *is* a reunion."

"Not for me, it isn't. There's nobody in this room under forty. Although I know you're probably helping out here."

"You can be my excuse for not hanging around," I say. "Believe me, there's plenty of reuning ahead — I have lots of time to help out."

We slip through the crowd and head for the stairs up to the lobby, but not before Essie Sue sees us. I wave and point to Josh, and then we're out of there before we see how she takes it. Joshie's rented a car, so I'm spared the return bus trip, too, as if I needed anything more to be thankful for.

As we drive, one part of me listens to the details of his flight, but the other part is distracted by thoughts of grocery lists, figuring out what I don't have in the refrigerator that Joshie likes. He says he's had dinner, and that food's the last thing on his mind. This doesn't cut it with me as his mother — I know how much he can eat while protesting he's not hungry. And amazingly, none of it puts fat on him — not fair. He's wiry like Stu was, but with red hair like my side of the family. Straight and thick, but brighter than my dark red curls, Joshie's hair has that sleek look I wish mine had. I have to keep my locks cut short or they're totally out of control.

He drives a lot faster than I do, but my presence apparently holds him to the speed limit on the freeway. Josh is a pretty energetic guy, but he seems exceptionally keyed up tonight. We're home in no time, and as usual, he heads to the backyard to see Oy Vey, who adores him. She runs right over to him and tries to put her front paws on his shoulders. He's so tall she only makes it to his chest.

I use the garage entrance and then let the two of them in from the backyard through the sliding glass door. Immediately, Oy Vey lets out something between a light growl and a low whine.

"I've never heard that combination before," I say.

Josh is answering me, but I can't hear what he's saying. What I do hear is a much more shrill whine that's pitched like a siren. It's not coming from Oy Vey.

"Uh, I think that's my surprise making the racket," Josh says.

I turn in the direction of the noise, and see a blue plastic cage in the entrance hall.

"Meet Chutzpah," he says, stooping to lift out a diminutive orange tabby emitting a blast much too large for his body.

"He followed Claire and me home from the beach," Joshie tells me, "and he apparently made us an offer we couldn't refuse. We tried giving him to her neighbor because Claire's pet parakeet hates him, but he wouldn't stay over there. He insisted on belonging to us."

"And your own apartment doesn't take pets, as I recall."

"I tried to sneak him home, but he was too loud to conceal. The manager told me it was him or me."

"It's pretty clear you're making *me* an offer I can't refuse," I say.

"He's neutered."

"Thanks for small favors. But what's Oy Vey going to think? I haven't had another animal here in years, and you know how spoiled she is. She's used to all my attention."

"Can you keep him and see how it works out, Mom?"

"Only if you make me a promise. If Chutzpah and Oy Vey don't get along, I'll try to find him a home, and if I don't, you have to take him back and make the rounds up in Wilmington Beach. That's the only way I'll take him — otherwise, it's too big a responsibility."

"It's a deal." I see his face relax, but I'm not letting him get by with it quite yet.

"You are staying around for Chutzpah's transition period, aren't you? I've got the reunion this week, and I can't be here to protect Oy Vey."

"I'll be here all week to help them get used to each other. But why do you assume it'll be Oy Vey who needs protecting? She's ten times as big as he is."

"You're joking, right?"

I direct his attention to our beautiful golden retriever, who's cowering under the coffee table as the teensy kitty hurls high-pitched leonine howls at her.

"You've got to admit he's cute, Mom." Joshie's trying hard.

"Only if these decibels don't go on all night," I tell him.

Chutzpah *is* cute, actually. He has this pixielike head and gold eyes. But as usual, I'm not anxious to show what a pushover I am. Josh's face tells me how relieved he is — his look reminds me of the way he was as a little kid when he thought he had it made but wasn't quite sure. Of course, in those days he always had his dad to back him up, and thinking about that brings tears to my eyes. Faced with the two of them, I didn't stand a chance, and of course they both knew my weak spot when it came to strays.

I try to pick up the kitty, but he's having none of it — he's too busy stalking his gigantic prey. So instead, I get on my knees by the coffee table and reach out my arms to Oy Vey, who appreciates it and ventures out as far as my lap. I just cleaned the carpet — I guess that's now a lost cause with the new kitten. In this older neighborhood, upkeep is a necessity, whether it works or not.

"The name you've chosen for this cat is

not lost on me," I say, still unwilling to concede so easily. "He's certainly got balls."

"Not anymore," he assures me.

6

The worst thing about this reunion is my having no home base in Austin. Riding back and forth is bad enough, but once I'm at the hotel, I have no place to relax — I'm always *on*. I didn't spend the money to rent a room, and like most of the unmoneyed congregants, I go back to Eternal at night to sleep. Now that Joshie is visiting, of course, I have good reason to want to be home, not that I'm getting much rest here in Eternal. Last night was pure hell. Chutzpah never shut up, even though Oy Vey wisely demanded to sleep in the backyard instead of his usual roost at the foot of my bed. To his credit, Joshie took over as he had promised, but I still heard all his ups and downs. It's amazing how much havoc a creature that tiny can create.

Of course, the possibility of sleep apnea is on my mind, too. When they called and told me there was a cancellation at the testing center for this Saturday night, I grabbed it. I'm sure I'll be sick of Essie Sue's reunion by then, and this is not something I want to neglect. And my

Sunday night will still be free for the big reunion banquet.

The doorbell interrupts my delicious nap on the sofa this afternoon, sounding much more like the buzzer that it is than anything so soothing as to contain the word *bell*. I jump up and stagger to the door. It's Kevin — wearing his black dress suit and wing tips.

"Why aren't you ready, Ruby? Essie Sue wants us to be in Austin early to help set up for the big givers' cocktail party."

"You're dressed already?"

"Yeah. Essie Sue's taking one bus up early with the committee. She asked you to come up on that bus, too, remember?"

I let him in while I get my bearings — I'm still not quite coherent.

"It's time already? I can't believe it — I just curled up on the sofa a few minutes ago."

Well, it obviously wasn't only a few minutes ago. I must have been sleeping for an hour and a half. I'll never make it to the bus, even with Kevin's help.

"Let's just take your car, Kevin."

"Okay, you can use me as an excuse for not making it," he says. "Tell Essie Sue I had car trouble. She'd be furious if she thought you'd overslept."

I give him a grateful look and head upstairs. How can this man be so unaware one minute, and so canny the next? I guess the one almost mandates the other when you live life inside Kevin's skin.

Halfway upstairs, I remember that Joshie's home. I turn around and go down to the kitchen to find him. Since our kitchen's always been the center of the house, it's always the first place I look. He's left a note on the big table in the middle of the room — his usual MO from years back.

> *Mom . . .*
> *Chutzpah and I have given you and Oy Vey a rest — we'll be at Roy Kaplan's apartment if you need us. I'll pass on the reunion for tonight, and will probably stay here for the night. Have fun. Love.*

Nuts — his first full day home and his friend Roy's the one who gets to visit with him. I guess it's one less thing to worry about, although I still wish he'd picked a different weekend to come in. I suspect his return had more to do with Chutzpah, of course, than with homesickness, but I've learned to enjoy his trips on any terms.

I jump in the shower, then throw on a

pair of velvet pants, a dressy top, and some good jewelry, and race Kevin to his car all in the space of fifteen minutes. I'd like to see anyone beat that record, but of course most people wouldn't be inclined to, not at the expense of the little niceties like makeup and a primped hairdo.

When we get to Austin, it's early. No one has asked me to do anything specific, and I'm certainly not volunteering. When Kevin goes off to find Essie Sue, I decide to take an hour for myself before going into party mode.

The hotel is a place transformed. The KillerCon convention people have moved in and taken over — many hundreds of them. There are lines for everything — registration, restaurants, panels, and parties. Sneakers and sweatpants are in the majority, making the dressed-up Temple Rita reunioners I catch sight of look like holdovers from a Don Ameche movie — not that it matters, because our relatively small bunch is lost amid the hordes.

Although our reunion group can hold its own in the weird department, some of these mystery people look pretty mysterious to me. There are the casuals who'd obviously rather be sitting down reading a book, the purposeful trader types, who seem to be stalking certain queen bees for appointments, and the wanderers, who look lost — I think those are the panel authors. I'm accosted in vain by four of them who appear to be looking for their moderator.

In one of the many bars, a white-bearded man in a giveaway cowboy hat lets me take a look at his convention directory. Just as I'm about to see if any of my favorite authors is here, Kevin runs up to the tiny cocktail table where I'm sitting. He's holding a handkerchief to his mouth.

"Ruby, you have to help me. I bit down on something hard — maybe it was the shell of a nut — and I think I broke a tooth. The area's bleeding, too. And I can only talk out of the right side of my mouth."

"I'm sorry, Kevin. Is it numb or does it hurt?"

"It's killing me. Here." I wrapped what he handed me in a tissue. "Keep it in your coat pocket and drive me to the dentist?"

"You mean now?" I'm a bit disoriented by Kevin's arrival, but I remember to hand the directory back to the guy at the next table.

"Yeah, I think we should go to Dr. Pascal's office — you know him. I had to come up to Austin to have him put in that special tooth."

I know Mort Pascal well. He does a bit more than the general dentistry practiced in Eternal, and I've had to use his services many times.

"Hurry, Ruby. You should drive because if I try to keep both hands on the steering wheel, I won't be able to hold the handkerchief up to my mouth and keep the blood from dripping on my new shirt."

Before I know it, I'm in Kevin's car, driving on my least favorite Austin freeway. I call ahead on my cell and alert the office just as they're ready to close.

The receptionist is halfway out the door for home as soon as she lays eyes on us — I'm glad I warned her we were coming. She waves us toward the examining rooms, and Mort Pascal greets us in the hallway.

"What's up, Rabbi?"

I can tell that the receptionist isn't the only one in a hurry to get out of here before five-thirty. Mort's looking at his watch as he leads Kevin to the dentist chair, and he sticks his hand in Kevin's mouth without waiting for an answer to his question.

"You sure broke a big chunk of the tooth," he says. "I'll numb this out for you and put in a medicated fix on a temporary basis. You'll have to come back after the weekend. The tooth's been filled so many times it might need a crown at this point."

"Give him what I bit on, Ruby."

"Later," Mort says. "The needle's already in his mouth."

I'm not sure I'm even supposed to be in here watching, but since it's after hours, Mort seems oblivious. Oh well — if the dentist doesn't care how the tooth was broken, I suppose I can suppress my own natural curiosity for a while.

"Go in the waiting room, Ruby. This'll take a while."

So much for Mort's oblivion. The waiting room's quiet, and Kevin's asked me to call Essie Sue to tell her where he is. I thought he'd *been* with her all along.

"The rabbi picked now to break a tooth? We're here waiting for both of you, Ruby. Now he won't be able to address the fund-raising party."

I don't bother pointing out to Essie Sue that no one picks a time to break a tooth. I can't get through to her in most circumstances, much less on the eve of a big fund-raiser, so I quit trying.

"We'll be there when we can." I get off the phone before I have to say something about her compassion. Although if I'd stayed on longer, maybe I could have at least found out what Kevin was doing when he broke the tooth.

"*I'm rerry,* Ruby." That's Kevin lurching into the waiting room, followed by Mort. Now he *really* can't talk. He points to his chest, but I have no idea what he means.

"He's saying he's ready and he didn't get any blood on his shirt," Mort tells me. I guess after twenty years, a dentist can understand Novocaine-speak better than I can.

"Do you still want to go to the party?" I ask.

Kevin nods his head yes. He'd obviously prefer partying with a miserable mouth all night to risking Essie Sue's wrath by not showing.

7

When we get back to the hotel, I see Hal Margolis, Essie Sue's husband, in the lobby. Apparently, he's been sent to look for us. Hal's usual dour countenance, perfectly understandable considering whom he's lived with for forty years, seems overlaid with more than the usual stress tonight. Hal and I are unspoken pals even though the friendship isn't exactly overt. He's comfortably retired, but I've heard his investments have taken a beating lately, so I figure that's why he looks so distressed. I'm wrong.

"Hi, Ruby. And, Rabbi." Hal's never been able to relate to Kevin, but he tries. "Since we had a couple of hours to spare before the big cocktail party, Essie Sue's invited some of the temple volunteers up to our suite on the third floor. She wants you to come up."

"Uh-oh," Kevin says. Then he remembers he can't move his lips very easily. "Am I late? Is she . . ."

"He promised to help set up the special favors Essie Sue has for the big givers," I tell Hal, explaining about the quick trip to the dentist.

"Don't worry about it," Hal says, "it's early yet. And she has other things on her mind."

"What other things?" I say.

"She got into a big argument with Freddie Fenstermeister, that son of a bitch. He booked the Presidential Suite for himself, and Essie Sue had to take whatever was left after the KillerCon people were set up. She wasn't too happy."

The man's a master of understatement, and I'm suddenly thankful we haven't been around the last couple of hours. We follow Hal through the corridors to the elevator. A line of people a block long is waiting to go up.

"I can't take this," I say. "Let's use the stairs."

Kevin's visibly unhappy at this suggestion, but he can't say much in protest, so he goes along.

"Freddie can't stand us, you know," Hal says as we climb the stairs. "He's always been jealous of Essie Sue's leadership in the Temple. He thinks the top spot is his due because his family founded the place, but she's earned it and he hasn't."

"So what else is new?" I say. "This has

been going on for years."

"He's done a couple of dirty deals against me financially, too, Ruby. And they cut us off socially in certain circles."

"I'm sorry, Hal. Maybe you can just get through the reunion and go back to ignoring him."

I can hear crowd noises through the half-open door at the end of the hall.

"Hal, honey, I thought you'd never get here." Essie Sue reaches up to kiss Hal on the cheek.

"Ruby, this was no time to keep the rabbi away from his reunion obligations."

Kevin is frantically making mouth gestures that his tooth is broken. Essie Sue is unmoved.

"I'm sorry, Rabbi," she says. "But I'm sure someone in the hotel could have fixed you up in a jiffy."

"They don't keep hotel dentists on call, Essie Sue," I say. "Be glad he made it here at all. And, besides, Kevin gave you lots of help earlier before he broke his tooth."

Kevin's nodding appreciatively. It's the least I can do to try to ease Essie Sue's wrath, but she's not pacified.

"All I asked him to do was to go down to the reception room and take a picture of my State of Texas chopped liver mold in the ice chest before all those people mess it up."

"It *is* edible, right?" I ask. "They're supposed to eat it."

"Well, they don't have to be pigs about it before everyone has a chance to admire the workmanship."

Lots of luck trying to tell our people that they can't get to the chopped liver, but I don't bother pointing that out.

"Why did you decide to have a preparty party up here in your suite anyway, Essie Sue?"

Hal answers for her. "She was giving the chefs so much grief they told her they were going to close the reception room for the fifteen minutes before the event so she couldn't change anything else. She had plenty of time to kill."

"Not true," Essie Sue says. "I'm hosting this little bash because the Fenstermeisters have been entertaining in their suite since the reunion began, and I wanted to show them that they're not the only ones who can be hospitable."

From the look on Hal's face as we order our drinks, he's thinking that Essie Sue's little bash is going to cost him plenty.

8

It takes a while for Essie Sue to coax all of us — a whole room full of people — two floors upstairs from her suite to the official reception. Most are holding out for the main elevators — a ten-minute wait at the very least — and some smarties discover a less-used service elevator down the hall. I take the stairs. At least the cocktail party's not too many floors up — that much of a jock I'm not.

Strangely, the big double doors to the reception room are still closed when we get there. We're met by a contingent who've come down from Freddie and Francie's preparty in the Presidential Suite. After Essie Sue bombards the front desk on her cell, one of the headwaiters shows up to let us into the room.

The few big givers who haven't been wined and dined by either Freddie or Essie Sue also join the ranks, and true to form, Essie Sue still insists on having all guests show their invitations to her appointed gatekeepers before entering. We're right up front.

"She knows everyone here," Kevin mumbles to me at the door. He's still not getting his words out easily, and I can hardly understand him. "Wouldn't you say this identification process is overkill, Ruby?"

"So what else is new?"

"Maybe she thinks it makes us feel special and important," he says.

"Don't attribute her needs to the rest of us," I say. "I didn't even keep my invitation, and from the looks of it, neither did anyone else. Let her try to keep us out."

Alice Gold and Brad Fine, the lucky invitation takers, are being overwhelmed by the reunion guests behind us, who are obviously tired of milling around outside the room.

"Forget it, Essie Sue," I hear Hal tell her, "just stand aside and let them in."

Kevin and I are pushed along with the tide.

I pull him with me. At least with Kevin I don't have to make small talk.

"I don't know about you," I say, "but I'm hungry. Let's go try the renowned chopped liver."

"And mess it up?" he says.

"I assume you got a good photo of the State of Texas in its pristine state for Essie

Sue to frame," I say. "From now on, the liver's public land. Consider that we're homesteading."

"I don't know, Ruby. Essie Sue might be mad if we're the first. I want to stay away from it. You go. It's behind that curtain."

"Behind the curtain? I'm not *that* hungry — maybe Essie Sue has something planned."

I can't believe Kevin looks this nervous — I thought he'd made progress controlling that raw fear Essie Sue inspires in the uninitiated. Maybe he's just hurting.

We're spared the *who-goes-first* routine as Essie Sue pushes past us with an empty glass and a spoon in her hand. She waves at an extremely uncoalesced crowd still entering the room, and bangs on the glass. It doesn't help.

"People — people, pay attention. This is a party and not the time for speech making. We'll do that at Temple. I do, however, want our most devoted and illustrious contributors to be aware of the loving care I have put into my legendary, I might even say famous, State of Texas chopped liver mold. It's almost a shame to disturb it."

"Give us a break, Essie Sue," Bubba Copeland yells out. By now the crowd has settled down to a noise level beyond ear-splitting. "You didn't set it in cement, did you?"

"I'll graciously ignore that, Bubba, considering the source. And *au contraire,* it's delicious besides being historic and artistic. My loving husband Hal helped me with the chopping and the schlepping — as well as graciously transporting the liver mold from our kitchen in Eternal to the hotel here in Austin. Hal and I are also exhibiting the antique brass mortar and pestle my great-grandmother used in the old country to prepare some of the ingredients."

"So where's the big deal?"

"You're spoiling the presentation, Bubba. Shut up."

With that oh-so-gracious addendum, Essie Sue opens a curtain pulled across a raised platform.

"See," I whisper to Kevin, "we won't be the first ones. Someone's already examining the chopped liver."

It's the man with the green plaid pants. I haven't seen him since the first gathering, and I still don't know who he is or who brought him.

This guy's awfully intent on that buffet platter, and if he negotiated his way behind the curtain to be first, I'm thinking he'd better dig in pronto. With this crowd, you don't get a second chance.

It only takes me a minute to realize that nobody could be that interested in chopped liver. Either that, or he's near-sighted to the point of being half-blind. He's standing close up to the table, bent at the waist, with his head down to the level of the platter.

"Excuse me," Essie Sue says. "Can I help you? We have a national treasure here, and we need to make way so everyone can enjoy."

Uh-oh. The man in the green plaid pants is definitely beyond help. His slender body is squarely folded forward waist-high, with his chest draped across the width of the table, precariously balanced as if his legs were still holding him up. His head is facedown, buried deep in the large mound of crushed ice covering the platter where Essie Sue's celebrated State of Texas chopped liver mold was supposed to be. Or used to be. It's gone.

9

Essie Sue is at first frozen to the spot, with the curtain pull still in her hand. Then she turns to the buffet — not laying a hand on the stranger in the plaid pants. Simply bumping the table, though, is all the motion it takes to dislodge his body, which slides to the floor, taking the silver base and all the ice with it.

"Where's my chopped liver sculpture? And who is this man?" she asks in that order.

I'm not surprised that Essie Sue in a state of shock is as tactless as Essie Sue in her everyday incarnation, but I suppose we should be grateful she mentioned the dead man at all.

The crowd is pushing forward — at least, those of us who can see what's happening. Most people, still clueless, are making conversation and no doubt wondering why our speechmaker-in-chief has fallen silent. Or relatively so, and not for long.

"This is the man," she says, "who was milling around at our welcoming reception. I went over to ask him to fill out a name tag, but I lost him in the crowd and never saw him again."

That echoes my experience — I meant to go talk to him or ask someone, but then Joshie came in, and I forgot about everything. The man must have had some sort of attack.

"Call a doctor — maybe he's fainted." That's a voice from the crowd, which is rapidly getting the message.

"Stay back, everyone," I hear myself saying, but certainly not so that this stranger can have a chance. His luck ran out some time ago, if I'm any judge of dead bodies.

Having said that, I'd be the last person to pronounce anyone dead, and we do need someone up here fast. Who knows — maybe I'm wrong. I dial 911 on my cell — if my prior experience with this establishment is any indication, it'll be a lot quicker than calling the front desk. My fingers are ready to speed dial Paul Lundy at the police station when I realize that's premature.

We don't have to wait at all, though, because Jack Baker, a pediatrician, is being pushed to the front of the room, where he soon confirms my hunch. He's kneeling in front of the body, and I can see him

63

shaking his head no when asked if the man's alive.

The buzz of who-is-he's in the room turns into silence as the realization sinks in that we've had a death here. Even Essie Sue is quiet — she's leaning on Hal's arm and Freddie Fenstermeister's brought up a chair for her — I guess trauma can inspire a truce now and then, however temporary.

It's a good thing Kevin doesn't have to give last rites — between the dentist visit and this, he's looking positively green.

I go up to Jack Baker and tell him I've called 911.

"Will they take care of the next steps?" I say.

"They'd better, Ruby," he says. "The man's sustained a blow to the back of his head."

I guess my instinct to call Paul Lundy wasn't so inappropriate after all. I pick up the phone to do just that. It can't hurt to have someone we feel secure with handling this from the beginning.

"I'm calling Lieutenant Lundy," I say.

"Who's he?" Jack asks me.

That's when I realize I'm calling Paul because he makes *me* feel secure.

I'm using his personal number, and I get him on the first ring.

"Paul, it's Ruby."

"Hi. What's up? You sound upset."

"We're in a mess here at the temple reunion."

I can practically hear him smacking his head — in a professional way, of course.

"That tone of voice usually means I'm in for a year's work," he says. "Where are you?"

"In Austin."

I suddenly realize this isn't even his jurisdiction.

"I'm sorry, Paul. My calling you was a knee-jerk reaction — I should have known this was something the Austin police would handle. I'm sure in a few minutes I would have come to my senses — this just happened minutes ago — or I should say we discovered the body minutes ago. A man who was a stranger to us, but who was seen at one of our receptions earlier, was hit over the head and killed. That's all I know at this point."

"You said temple reunion, Ruby. So why aren't you at the Temple?"

"That's a long story — the reunion's being held here and in Eternal — we go back and forth on a bus, courtesy of the Margolis planning committee. It's been lots of fun commuting, as you can imagine."

"You have my condolences. On more than one front, I guess. But if you're looking for my involvement, you've probably got it. I doubt the investigation will go very far without the Temple Rita contingent here in Eternal being part of the case, Ruby."

"So this wasn't a total waste for you?"

"It's never a waste talking to you — you know that. I'm close with half the force up there. Just sit tight and I'll look into it. As long as emergency's on its way, let them call in the police. They know how to handle it."

I get off the phone as soon as I see the EMT crew come into the room and go over to the body. When I apologize for bringing them here, they brush it off.

"It happens a lot," one of the women tells me, "a professional's not always available, so it's safer to call us than to leave someone unattended. My partner's calling the police now, and I'm sure they'll ask that everyone stick around until they get here."

The hotel security people are here, too — someone must have called downstairs. They're doing a pretty good job of calming the crowd, which doesn't include Essie Sue — her second wind has appeared, and she's badgering Kevin — to do what, I don't know.

"You've got to call the meeting to order, Rabbi. Use your authority."

"What?" He's looking at her as though she's totally lost it, which of course, she has.

"Well, this is a gathering for our reunion, whether you call it a meeting or not, and you're our spiritual leader. Do something."

He looks at me, but I'm having none of it. Okay, almost none of it.

"The rabbi just had some serious dental work," I say. "He can hardly talk, so don't count on him."

"I never count on him — that's the problem."

"Quit it, Essie Sue," I say. "You want everything back to normal. It ain't gonna happen, so don't take it out on Kevin. Go bother your cochairman."

To my surprise, she does just that.

"Freddie, do something. Your family's being honored tonight."

"My family's being honored all weekend," he says, taking his wife's arm. "I can wait. I'm taking Francie and returning to the suite — there's no comfortable place to sit down in here."

"Wait," she says. "Did you see this man

last night when he was milling around?"

"No, did you?"

"Yes, but I didn't find out who he was."

"He doesn't look like one of us," Francie says. "Those green plaid pants belong on a golf course, not at a fancy reception."

The police have arrived, and their main problem seems to be keeping people out, not in. One of the officers comes up to Essie Sue.

"I hear you're in charge," he says.

"Yes," she says, accepting her due.

"We understand most of you are connected with the Temple down in Eternal. We're trying to break the crowd into smaller groups right now. But who are these other people in the back of the room?"

The word has obviously leaked out to the KillerCon convention. I go to the back and see a dozen people rushing through the double doors before they're shut. Half of them are ready to take notes, and the other half are carrying tape recorders.

I recognize a budding mystery author from an Austin book group, and she loses no time in recruiting me.

"Ruby Rothman — I thought that was you I saw. I need an *in*, before everyone else gets here. Can you show me the body?"

"Huh?"

She waves her notebook.

"Research, darling, research."

I could tell her this isn't a living lab, but I give up when we both hear Essie Sue asking the officer in charge to add a count to the murder investigation.

"There have been two offenses committed here," she says. "The first is murder, and the second is theft."

"What are you talking about, lady?"

"I've been trying to tell everyone. My State of Texas chopped liver mold has been stolen."

10

I sleep exactly two hours early this morning after escaping back to Eternal when the police finish questioning us at the hotel. I was wired from all the commotion, so I calmed down by e-mailing Nan and telling her about the killing before I faded from exhaustion. I've never been so happy to fall into my bed safe and sound, which is why my doorbell ringing at 8 a.m. sharp is such an unwelcome intrusion. In denial mode whenever possible, I crawl farther under the covers and ignore the insistent buzz. It works.

At least until — not quite unconscious again, I hear creaking on the stairs leading up to my room. That's always an eye-opener. I'm thinking this is something Essie Sue would pull if she had a key or knew how to break in. But she doesn't, on both counts. It's not Joshie, because he's at his friend's house. By now, of course, I'm fully awake and ready for any old ax murderer who happens to drop by Watermelon Lane at breakfast time.

"Ruby, are you there? Are you awake, honey?"

It's Ed's voice, which solves most but not all of the puzzle since he has a key. Why is he up from San Antonio at this time of the day? I usually love seeing him, but I have to admit I'm less than thrilled to be surprised in my gargoyle-like state, even if he's no stranger to the early-morning me. After all, there's a difference between his waking up to my tousled locks on the pillow and his barging into the real me on two hours' sleep.

"What are you doing here?" is all I can manage to croak.

"Great to see you, too, honey."

Oh no. Not chipper. I hate chipper.

He kisses me on the end of one of my sticking-out bunches of hair and then plops on the foot of the bed, disturbing Oy Vey's sleep, too. She doesn't seem to mind as much as I do, but then, she gets petted and I don't.

"What's up?" I say. Not gracious, sexy, or girlfriendish, I admit, but hey, at least the words are in the right order.

"You're grouchy this morning."

I don't bite. I'm still annoyed that he hasn't been here much lately. "I thought you were so busy at the paper, you couldn't come up."

"I think I can stay for the day."

I'd love to have him for the weekend, especially after what's happened. I'm so exhausted my mind's in shreds, and having Ed here would make it so much easier to cope.

"Do you think you could make it for a little longer?" I say, loosening up a bit. Looking at him does that to me. "You can't imagine everything that happened last night."

"You mean the guy with his head in the ice? How in the world did he get himself in that position if . . ."

He's slipping into interview mode, but thinks better of it after taking one look at the expression on my face.

"Yeah," he says, "we heard about it already."

"Which is why you're here bright and early."

"I knew you were going to say *I told you so* — that if I'd been here for those reunion nights like you wanted, I'd have been in on this from the beginning."

"No, hon, I really wasn't interested in gloating over your missed opportunity. It wasn't your story I was thinking about at all. It was about priorities, but I can see you don't get that."

"Look, I just thought if I started with

you, I could get an angle I couldn't get with the hotel or the police. You've got to admit, it's right in our laps, so to speak. How could you want me to pass that up?"

"You knew the police wouldn't release that much this soon, and you were hoping I would, right?"

"I can't believe you wouldn't want to help me."

Maybe it is unfair of me. How many journalists could ignore a story that was as close as their own girlfriend? Since I don't know enough about the events of last night to spill anything, I might as well give him background.

"Off the record," I say. "I'll just give you my take on what happened — at this point, I don't know fact from speculation."

"Thanks, honey."

Now I know it's all business. He's not even annoyed with me on general principles now that he's getting what he came for.

"Don't I even get my coffee?" I say. "I'll meet you in the kitchen."

I can smell the fresh coffee he's made when I'm barely out of the shower. Since I'm unfortunately not going to be conducting the interview in bed, I go downstairs in jeans, sneakers, and a favorite baby pink cable-knit sweater that for me is the visual equivalent of comfort food.

"I hope you made a whole pot," I say.

"That and your bagel half. I remembered the Dundee Marmalade, too."

He kisses me as if he'd just walked in, and I put my responses on hold, something I've done a lot of lately.

I fill him in on the discovery of the body while I'm swilling down the first mug. Black.

"Do they have any clue as to who did it?"

"Not that they told me. You have to remember that I don't know the Austin police — Paul Lundy wasn't there. I did call him, though, to alert him."

"You called him before the Austin people did?"

"Yep. On my cell."

"So why didn't you call me?"

"It never occurred to me, Ed. You weren't even in town."

"Neither was he."

I guess he has me there. "No, but I was thinking police, and to tell you the truth, I forgot it wasn't his jurisdiction."

Ed and Paul aren't exactly friends, and since Paul's an old buddy of mine and we talk a lot, I'm not always so forthcoming about every little conversation. But this morning, I don't feel like worrying about it.

"Did they split everyone up for interviews?"

"Brief ones, yes. Remember, they had a room full of people, most of whom were there from Eternal for the evening, and the rest from out of town. And literally no one knew this guy, so we weren't much help. I'm sure that if this had taken place in a couple of days, after we had some of the workshops Essie Sue planned, we'd have known who he was."

"Could be that he was only there in the crowd, and that he wouldn't have appeared for the more personal gatherings."

"True enough. I told you I don't know much."

"Did they collect any evidence?"

"They blocked off the area pretty quickly, and I saw some collection going on with baggies and stuff. But Essie Sue had just opened the curtain when we saw him, and I didn't have a chance to see what else was on the table. Just food, I guess."

"What's next?"

"They told those of us not staying in Austin that we could take the bus or our cars back home to Eternal, but that we were supposed to let them know where we were. That should be no problem, since everyone's here for the reunion."

"You mean you're continuing it?" he says.

"Yeah. Essie Sue's adamant that we continue, and I think the cops would prefer keeping the group together."

"It's weird though, still celebrating."

"Nothing planned by Essie Sue turns out to be very celebratory, Ed, and as far as weirdness is concerned, what else is new? Her point was that since this was a complete stranger to everyone in the room, it would be weird *not* to continue with the reunion until we find out more. He could have just wandered in from the street both nights."

"Not likely.

"So you haven't heard anything about what the police think? Can't Paul help you?"

"I think what you're saying, Ed, is can Paul help *you?* You seem to be the one in need of fast information. Why don't you call Paul yourself?"

"He doesn't much like me, for openers."

"You know, I've given you as much as I have, which admittedly isn't much, but I did tell you all of it. Aside from my becoming the reporter instead of you, what else do you want from me?"

This really pisses me off, and he knows it. We've worked on things before where we've both been involved in the outcome, but this makes me feel *used* in an entirely different way. He's up here just to get this story out of me. And what's especially galling is that last week when I asked him to go to the reunion with me, he couldn't be bothered.

"Okay, Ruby, I can see I went too far. But at least keep an eye open for me, will you, hon? Even if you just get some ideas on which direction the case is taking."

"Ed, I can't even speculate. Maybe we'll learn more later today. The congregants in Eternal are giving the reunion guests home hospitality until tomorrow — I got out of hosting someone when Josh surprised me with a visit. A friend of mine doubled up and took my guest.

"All the reunion people are being bused down here today for tours of whatever's new in Eternal, and tonight we're having a special service at Temple. Afterward, we're having some sort of twenty questions Truth or Consequences' session, where everyone's supposed to tell what they've done in the last twenty years."

"Telling your secrets, huh?"

"Yes, you can guess whose idea that was."

I'm feeling *iffy* about this program — hope it goes well. Secrets can be dangerous.

11

E-mail from: Nan
To: Ruby
Subject: *Only You*

It's a good thing I'm used to you or I'd think you were weird, girl. Only you would e-mail me, then phone to say you were sending another e-mail. So why did you want me to stand by?

E-mail from: Ruby
To: Nan
Subject: *Here It Is*

Sorry for the delay in writing this, babe. I'm crazed this morning because everything's happening at once, and I need your calming presence again, even if it's only your virtual presence.

Ed showed up here at eight this morning. Believe me, this was the least of my expectations — he never drops in early anymore — he's only late or missing in action. But there he was, pumping me for information about the killing as if I owed him. I did great while he was here — told him exactly what I thought, but after he left, I felt lousy.

I don't know how I'm going to talk to Paul about any new information while dodging Ed. I'm positive the police won't want the press to speculate when they've barely begun to investigate. On the other hand, I was angry this morning and ruined any chance of romance, if that's what Ed had in mind for later.

E-mail from: Nan
To: Ruby
Subject: *Listen to Your Head and Not Your Hormones*

I know I'm the last one you'd expect this advice from, but take stock, Ruby. Ed gave you no notice whatsoever. Just help the police when asked — and forget about Ed's scoops. He's obviously not worried about your schedule.

E-mail from: Ruby
To: Nan
Subject: *As If My Hormones Remember Why They're Here at This Point*

You're right, of course. It's just that the prospect of having Ed here today was such a rarity I wanted to be able to enjoy it. We've had so little time together. I'm also feeling guilty about the prospect of keeping things from him.

E-mail from: Nan
To: Ruby
Subject: *Don't Be*

You're always a little soft in the head when it comes to Ed, and I can understand that. But this isn't the time, Ruby. You know he wouldn't have any qualms about keeping something from you if it were for professional reasons. So do what you have to do and worry about him later. If you shake him up a little, maybe it'll be better for the relationship, not worse.

E-mail from: Ruby
To: Nan
Subject: *I Hear You*

Okay, I'm helping Paul as needed and bagging the guilt. But just like me to fall for a journalist, huh?

P.S. This isn't the first time you've kicked me in the pants — thanks.

E-mail from: Nan
To: Ruby
Subject: *Thatagirl*

This is the Ruby I know. Go for it.

12

When I see Kevin coming to the pulpit wearing his white robes, I know we're in for a long night.

"He's wearing those as a special favor to me," Essie Sue tells me as we file into reserved seats in the first row of the Temple. As usual on these occasions, I'm representing ghosts of rabbis past, because of my unique status as Stu's widow. I still miss him every day of my life, and especially when I walk in here — even though the place is totally different now that Kevin's the rabbi.

"I thought those white robes were only hauled out on the High Holy Days," I say to Essie Sue.

"Well, there's no rule they can't be worn at other times, Ruby. I felt our big givers deserved the formality."

Joshie, sitting beside me in a sport jacket and tie that he actually put on voluntarily, rolls his eyes, although he's never had a problem with Essie Sue. As a preacher's kid, as he likes to call himself, he learned early on to go into neutral around the more difficult congregants and let his mom and dad do the dealing. I'm relieved he wasn't turned off his heritage altogether, but he seems to have worked out his own approach to Judaism with a little help from his friends and a lot of leeway from his parents.

"Are you okay?" he asks. He's probably the only one here tonight who knows how hard it is still for me to be in the sanctuary. Too many memories and too little current consolation. I squeeze his hand.

"You?" I say.

"I'm glad I decided to come along," he says. "It's been a while."

I know it's hard for him, too, and that he wanted to help me get through the weekend. I hope he's still pleased he came by the end of the evening. If past special occasions are any indication, I have my doubts — things always seem to implode when Kevin's feeling pressured.

The rows just behind us are reserved for the same people who were invited to the special cocktail party. I couldn't talk Essie Sue into a more democratic arrangement, and frankly, I didn't try very hard. The lucky reunion honorees are all shell-shocked after last night's disaster, anyway, and I don't think they're in any shape to protest something as banal as priority seating.

The Temple's full, something that usually terrifies Kevin, and I can see from his face that tonight's no exception. Besides, any sermonizing he does later will pale in comparison to what's happened in real life, and I'm sure he hasn't had time to rewrite his presentation. Mix that with a broken tooth and the result ain't gonna be pretty.

I look at the program and realize Kevin's not the only one preaching — he and Essie Sue have anointed three representatives from the reunion to give sermonettes — all are alliteratives, I notice — Larry Lowry for the over fifties, Betty Behr for the over forties, and Clementine Cohen for the over thirties. No one under thirty showed up, unless you count Joshie, who flew down for reasons having more to do with his cat than with old times. *After that,* Kevin's preaching — *oy.* We're in for a long, long evening.

Services are also led by the visitors — a mixed blessing, I always feel. You'd think they'd ask the participants to read at least a short passage first as a tryout, but for obvious reasons, I guess that's too awkward. As a result, the congregation is subjected to a variety of punishments — one voice so faint that even the microphone can't pick it up, another reading in a complete monotone, and a third by someone who hasn't gone over the part and stumbles at all words over two syllables. By the time the sermonettes have begun, Joshie and I have already eyed each other six or seven times. It doesn't get any better.

Larry Lowry, spokesman for the over half-century people, is not only way over seventy (Essie Sue prefers to cast all seniors such as herself as merely over fifty) but he's been an accountant in Cleveland for the fifty years since he left Eternal. This circumstance doesn't enliven his talk by very much, and makes it painfully obvious that he hasn't done much public speaking during that time, either. We do learn that he's for the three "I's" — Israel, the Cleveland Indians, and his son Isadore, who's good with numbers.

Betty Behr, speaking for the over forties, assures us that the real Texans never depart the state. After leaving Eternal, she became a proud resident of Dallas, where she raised five children, none of whom married outside the faith, we're told. Those of us who know her realize that this accomplishment was made easier by the fact that only two of her children married at all, but she doesn't mention that.

Clementine Cohen from Lubbock says she's for the *thirtysomethings.* Make that *thirtyeverythings.* Clementine seems to think she's in some sort of competition with the other age groups, and spends her allotted time bragging about the accomplishments of the youngsters in the crowd. Her sermonette is like Essie Sue's Chanukah letter, and like every multirecipient Christmas epistle I've ever received. She enumerates each doctor, lawyer, and merchant in her group, and ends up with a rousing *hip, hip, hooray* for the overachieving over-thirties.

What's interesting to me is that none of the presenters talk about their days in Eternal and what life was like when they were growing up here. I'm thinking a little guidance might have been in order. Meanwhile, each speaker took twenty minutes, so a whole hour has passed, and we haven't even finished the service.

Kevin has an impossible task — no wonder he's looking like a doomed man. It would be nice if at least some mention was made about the reunion's significance, he should probably say something about the killing last night, and the bottom line is it's really getting too late for *any* speech-making. I don't envy him.

He solves everything by stepping up to the mike and pulling out a big sign from behind the lectern:

BROKEN TOOTH — CAN'T TALK MUCH.
SHALOM

An audible sigh rises from the room. Everyone's relieved to be released — except for Essie Sue, of course.

"I'm shocked," she says to us, "shocked. The rabbi was supposed to address us with the pièce de résistance, and impress all these dignitaries. Now he's botched it. Hal, honey, I think you should go speak to him. He seems to listen to you."

"Too late," Hal says. "The next reader's already gone up to begin the closing prayers. Ten more minutes and we're outa here. I could use a cup of coffee in the social hall."

"Really, Hal," Essie Sue whispers in a rasp you can hear six rows back, "you're so unspiritual. You're always wanting services to end. Our Oneg Shabbat in the social hall is supposed to be a reception celebrating the Sabbath, not a chance to stop praying."

"Uh-huh."

Hal, as taciturn as Essie Sue is loquacious, is usually miraculously able to cut her off and calm her when no one else can — at a price, though. What he suffers for living with her, only he can know.

13

A pretty shell-shocked group, having partaken of cake and decaf, forms a ragged semicircle in the Bloomberg Social Hall. Kevin, who I suspect can talk a teeny bit more than he's letting on, is taking full advantage of his disability by sitting in the back of the room, apparently veering between relief and agony. He doesn't have to lead the "Twenty Questions" session, but he does have to absorb the daggers Essie Sue's sending his way.

"We're calling this an 'Eighteen Question' session, people," she says, "because eighteen is *chai* in Jewish tradition, and *chai* is for life and luck. So forget the twenty. Understood?"

We all get it.

"Yeah, that means we can be out of here two questions sooner," Bubba Copeland says.

"You're welcome to leave, Bubba, if this reunion has no meaning for you. This will be a combination of 'Truth or Dare' and 'Twenty Questions' — I mean 'Eighteen.' I'm going to take the rabbi's place and ask each one of you questions about your life since you left Temple Rita. You must answer truthfully."

I guess that's the only resemblance to "Truth or Dare" or "Twenty Questions" we're going to get — we're in Essie Sue–land now. At least, though, we'll be able to hear from some of the reunion visitors. If she gives them a chance.

She doesn't. The game consists of asking each person's name, occupation, marital status, number of children, and place of residence. After about five of these, which sound dangerously like the sermonettes we've just heard, the reunioners rebel.

"Can't you do any better than this, Essie Sue?" Herb Sofar asks. "Pick someone and let people ask them whatever they like."

"All right," she says, "I'll yield to the group's wishes. I pick Marcie Ratner."

That's not surprising — Marcie's one of Essie Sue's best friends, who moved to Atlanta a year ago. Essie Sue probably figures she's relatively safe.

"Okay, Marcie," Essie Sue says. "What's the worst thing about your new temple that compares unfavorably with Temple Rita?"

Always nice to accentuate the positive. And anyway, Essie Sue was supposed to let someone else ask the question this time. Nobody notices, though, because they're all riveted, waiting for the answer.

"I have to think about this one," Marcie says.

Yeah, so would I. But she doesn't take long.

"It's too interactive," she says.

"What does that mean?" Brother Copeland, Bubba's twin, asks.

"Well, there's just too much give-and-take — it makes me nervous. Like, you know, in our Temple Rita services, how when the rabbi's talking, he's telling us things and we're listening?"

We all nod, since when a person talks, they're usually telling you something.

"Okay, when Rabbi Kapstein preaches, and he's standing up there and we're sitting down below, I feel real peaceful, like it's time to zone out and let my mind wander freely. My husband Bud falls asleep, but that's taking it too far. I just sort of rise out of myself."

"Like an out-of-body experience?" Louise Reiner asks.

"Yeah," Marcie says. "Temple Rita has a real cutting-edge type of service — not like in my new temple, where you can be rising out of yourself and suddenly you're called on to make some kind of remark about what the rabbi just said. Or you're asked to discuss something. It's embarrassing."

"Bummer." Louise Reiner looks toward the back of the room where Kevin is sitting, but he doesn't seem to realize he's being complimented. He's apparently having some sort of out-of-body experience himself, now that he's been relieved of leading the discussion.

"So what else is horrible at your new congregation, Marcie?" The crowd is warming up to this in a big way, and so is Marcie.

"Well, it's first-come, first-served at the High Holy Days, instead of like here, where if you're a member of the temple board or some other kind of big deal, your seat will be reserved for you. And you don't have to come early. I seem to *never* get there early. No one understands that when you're dressing three girls under twelve, one of them's going to lose her spangled ponytail holder or something and you have to find that under the car seat. Then you have to take the youngest down to the babysitting room and get her settled — then there's . . ."

Bubba Copeland's making a hook sign with his arm and glaring at Essie Sue.

"You're losing control of the meeting," he says. "I'm learning more than I ever wanted to. Why not turn things over to your cochairman?"

"Hear, hear." That comes from Francie Fenstermeister. She and Freddie, who's been squirming in his folding chair with a perpetual sneer on his face, look mad enough to spit.

"Didn't you say Freddie's supposed to be the cochairman of this reunion?" Herb says. "How come we never hear from him?"

"Because he hasn't done any work toward the event," Essie Sue says.

I'm expecting chair-throwing any minute, but the Fenstermeisters keep their composure. The crowd doesn't.

"Let's hear from Freddie."

"Quit taking over, Essie Sue."

"All right, people," she says, straining to quell the rebellion. "Let's get the meeting back on track."

I notice that Freddie's sneer has become a smirk. He seems tired, but it's hard to tell because of the well-groomed sheen that emanates from his person. He reminds me of so many moneyed men who have the best care they can buy, but then end up looking as if they're encased in Lucite. He says something to Francie, then stands up.

"Apparently, ladies and gentlemen, Mrs. Margolis and her illustrious husband can't stand to have anyone else in the limelight."

Hal jumps up and waves his fist. "Hey, you can come after me, but don't take out your spite on my wife."

"Take it easy, Hal," Herb says. "I didn't mean to start anything when I asked Essie Sue about Freddie. I forgot you two guys couldn't stand each other."

"Then let's have the women talk," Clementine Cohen from Lubbock says. "Essie Sue had a chance. How about you, Francie? Are you still collecting those Fabergé eggs?"

"One Fabergé egg, Clementine," Francie says, still obviously seething. "The same one Freddie gave me years ago."

"Well, whatever — it's still a knockout. I remember it from years back when you kept it in the glass cabinet in the middle of the room."

"It's still in a cabinet, but it was never in the middle of the room, Clementine."

Hal leans over to me. "Still bragging about their wealth," he says.

I wouldn't call that particular interchange *bragging* — it seemed to me that the Fenstermeisters got pulled into that discussion. Not that Hal's in any mood to distinguish. And I'm with Clementine — I've been in their home lots of times, and I remember a cabinet in the middle of the living room with a blue egg and a green one. Very expensive copies, I'm sure. Not that I'd dare get into this debate anyway.

"Thank you, Francie," Essie Sue says in a tone of voice that could cut shoe leather. "Our 'Eighteen Questions' session is coming to a close, and just for the record, I'm still in charge of the room. Are there any closing comments before I send everyone home?"

She has such a lovely way of putting things. I'm about to go find Joshie, who chose to look around the library after the Oneg instead of participating in our stunning interchange, when I see a hand in the back of the room.

It's Lieutenant Paul Lundy.

"This is our police department, people," Essie Sue says. "Did you have a question for us, Lieutenant?"

I've already headed back — Paul looks grim. Joshie's come in behind him — I guess Joshie senses something more interesting than ponytail holders.

"We want to see the Margolises, Ruby," Paul says in my ear. "Everyone else can go home — I gather you're winding up anyway?"

"Yes, we're finished, Paul." I wonder what the "we" means — then I see a couple of other men in the doorway.

"Since you're here," he says, "do you want to go tell Essie Sue, or shall I?"

"I'll do it."

Everyone's looking to see who's in the doorway. Too bad Essie Sue had to make a general announcement, or that Paul had to raise his hand. Now it'll all just call attention to matters that could have taken place after the crowd had been dismissed. I'm curious, too, of course — I don't like the look on Paul's face. I turn around and go back to where he's waiting.

"Hey, Paul, can't we get the people out of here first? I'm afraid they're not going to leave on their own now that you've been announced."

"Okay. I guess I didn't handle my entrance too well. Why don't you take Mr. and Mrs. Margolis to the rabbi's study? If I remember, the door over there leads to his corridor. We'll meet you there. That way, the crowd can disperse without all the fuss."

I go over to Essie Sue, who's still waiting in front of the room, and tell her the police

97

say she can wind up the meeting.

"Paul says there's nothing to report to the group, Essie Sue. He just wants you to continue bringing everything to a close, and then a few of us can stay behind to see what he needs."

I'm thinking it's best right now not to tell her whom he's asking to see.

"Well, I'm certainly staying, right?" Heaven forbid she's not in on everything.

"Of course. And the rabbi and I will stay, too. If you and Hal can slip away, we'll all meet in the study. But go ahead and conclude — the troops are getting antsy."

"Ladies and gentlemen," Essie Sue says, "our meeting has ended. The police have no update as yet for the reunion group — they're here on private business with a few of the leadership. Enjoy your hospitality with our families here in Eternal tonight. We have free time tomorrow so that you can all enjoy Shabbat in our hometown. We'll see you promptly tomorrow — Saturday night — for the bus trip from Eternal to Austin. There's an exciting evening planned, culminating in a traveling exhibition of Jewish ceremonial art."

I hear groans at that, but I'm much too interested in Paul's visit here to care.

The police seem to have disappeared

from the back of the room — I'm not sure where they are now that chairs are being scraped and everyone's milling around. It's a smart move, though, because now there's not a bottleneck at the back exit with people quizzing the detectives, and the room clears fairly quickly. I suppose relief at getting out of here has overcome most people's curiosity, especially now that Paul's said there are no new updates. But where's the self-proclaimed leadership? I'd think they would want to be included.

Oh, I remember why they're not around. The Fenstermeisters are having the Arrangements Committee over to their house tonight for a meeting and get-together after the temple event, and they must have left already to get ready for it. Kevin asked me to go with him, and I will if I can drag myself.

14

Joshie wants to see friends, and I let him have the car after I check with Paul to make sure he can give me a ride home if I'm tired.

"I could take you back to your house, Ruby," Kevin says on the way to his study, "if you don't end up going with me to the Fenstermeisters' tonight. You shouldn't have to come to your door in a police car. The neighbors might wonder if you're in trouble."

"My neighbors concluded I was trouble a long time ago," I tell him. "And I'm still enough of a kid to like riding in a police van, but I probably won't — Paul usually has his own car with him."

"Whatever. I'll bet Ed wouldn't like it."

"What Ed wouldn't like is the fact that he's gone back to San Antonio already, and is missing out on the latest murder case update, Kevin." Not very nice, but lately I haven't been feeling so charitable on this subject.

I'm not the only one with relationship problems — Oy Vey and his new housemate Chutzpah are still eyeing each other, and I'm dreading the time when Joshie leaves and I'm left to do the canine/feline counseling. Last time we left the house, we returned to find Oy Vey with a sore nose where Chutzpah had jumped up and bitten him. I really need this. Not to mention Oy Vey, whose only retaliation is to eat Chutzpah's cat food.

"Hey, Kevin," I say. "I just realized you're talking. What happened to the communication by Magic Marker? Has your mouth miraculously recovered?"

"It's not that I *couldn't* talk, Ruby. It's that I sounded odd, and I didn't want people making fun of me. Besides, all that dental work was exhausting. I was glad to get some time out — especially from all the Sturm und Drang of this weekend."

"You don't have to make excuses to me," I say. "But Essie Sue might be less than forgiving over your not preaching or leading the discussion."

"Well, now she's preoccupied with the murder. Who *was* that guy?"

"No one seems to know. We all thought someone else had brought him along — you know, someone's husband or boyfriend. I don't think anyone paid much attention."

We arrive at the study and find Essie

Sue, Hal, and the police already there. Paul has borrowed Kevin's rolling chair, the one I call the throne, and has moved it out in front of the desk. Essie Sue and Hal are on the sofa, and there are two more empty chairs for Kevin and me. Two of Paul's men are standing by the door, and they usher us in and point to the chairs.

"Do you mind if I use your armchair, Rabbi?" Paul says, more a statement than a question. I'm thinking he's wanting to make clear this is a meeting where the police are in charge, and it's working. Even the Margolises are compliant.

I know I should wait for an update, but I blurt out a question anyway.

"Have you identified the dead man?"

"His name is Max Cole. He has a criminal record, Ruby — that's all I can say right now."

"*He* has a criminal record?" Essie Sue says. "I thought the criminal was still at large. How could a criminal possibly be part of our group? Not that he *was* a part of our group, but you know what I mean, Lieutenant."

I've never seen her this flustered.

"I'm not here about the victim's identity, Mrs. Margolis, I'm here about the evidence we collected at the scene. We learned from our interviews that you own the antique brass mortar and pestle found on the table near the victim."

"Yes," Essie Sue says. "It's from my great-grandmother in Russia. She used it to grind ingredients for the wonderful chopped liver recipe I prepared for the reunion cocktail party. The liver that's disappeared, I might add. And we don't know where."

"But why did you bring the brass implements to the party?"

"As part of the exhibit, Lieutenant. This is a reunion — we're interested in our cultural heritage. I wanted people to see how the liver was originally made."

"Mr. Margolis, did you take part in the presentation?"

"Of course he didn't, Lieutenant. Hal helped me chop the liver, which has now disappeared, and he helped schlepp it in the car from Eternal to Austin. We brought the items for the exhibit, too — some letters in Yiddish from my great-grandmother to my grandmother, and a few family photos we never got to show because of this criminal who got killed."

I can see she's thoroughly accepted the idea now that the criminal must be responsible for his own murder.

Paul, looking pained but still very professional, gives me a quick glance and stands up.

"The victim was facedown in the crushed ice, as you know, but we also found traces of liver around his eyes and nose, indicating that the liver mold was probably resting on top of the ice at the time of death. It was removed after."

"Why?" Essie Sue asks. "Who stole it?"

"Unfortunately, Mr. Margolis," Paul says, looking at Hal and ignoring Essie Sue, "we've established that the heavy brass pestle you and your wife brought up to Austin was used to bash Max Cole's skull. Blood and hair found on the weapon match samples from the victim's head."

"Our family antique was the murder weapon?" Essie Sue says. "You must be mistaken."

Odd — Essie Sue still hasn't allowed Hal to answer for himself, but all Paul's remarks seem directed toward him. Paul doesn't appear to be concerned by this dichotomy one way or another. Maybe it doesn't matter.

I'm imagining what's coming next, but I can't really believe it.

"Mr. Margolis," Paul says, "these two men accompanying me are with the police up in Austin. Since I'm acquainted with you personally, I offered to arrange this meeting instead of having them contact you on their own, although the result will be the same. They'd like to take you to Austin now for questioning."

"Why?" I say. "What do you have, Paul?"

I feel I need to ask because Essie Sue and Hal have gone mute — Essie Sue's looking at Hal, and Hal seems to be in shock.

"Mr. Margolis's fingerprints are the only ones on the weapon," he says, "along with Max Cole's blood and hair. Unfortunately, that makes him a person of great interest to us."

"That's nonsense." Essie Sue has just barely found her voice. "My husband is of no interest to anyone. Hal didn't even know the man. I'd never seen him before, and if I don't recognize him, he doesn't."

"If Hal helped bring the brass items up from Eternal, of course his fingerprints are going to be on them," I say almost in desperation.

Hal, not looking at us, just sits there.

"This isn't the time for debating the case, Ruby," Paul says.

The two men position themselves on either side of Hal, and silently urge him up.

"I'm going, too," Essie Sue says.

"I don't think so," Paul answers, heading toward the door.

Then he hesitates and backtracks.

"All right, Mrs. Margolis, you can go, too. We may need you. And I've decided to come along."

On his way out of the room, Hal finally says something.

"I didn't lay a hand on the guy. Who is he?"

Before I can catch my breath, I'm sitting in the almost vacant study, looking around at the newly created space. Kevin's huge throne is empty in front of the desk, the sofa is bare, and he and I are side by side in our two pull-up chairs, staring at each other.

"This is unbelievable," I say. "They won't get anywhere."

"Don't be so sure, Ruby," Kevin says. "Those police meant business. What should we do?"

"You mean *now*, or what should we do about Hal's being under suspicion?"

"I mean about Freddie's meeting. That's where the committee is now, and where we're supposed to be."

"You probably need to go," I say. "Freddie'll want you there."

I'm ready to make my excuses and go home, but something doesn't feel right about that — I'm too keyed up to go to bed. Besides, I haven't had an invitation to Freddie's house since Stu died.

"Let's go," I say. "I'm coming with you."

15

As we step over the Fenstermeister threshold, I realize I prefer Essie Sue's type of pretentiousness. Her forays into home decor à la knockoffs from *Architectural Digest* may be untouchable to us ordinary mortals, but they're at least well planned, in an obsessive sort of way. She wouldn't be caught dead, for example, with the Western art that's rampant in every corner of Freddie's sprawling English Tudor home.

Wild horses even follow me as I make a quick detour into the guest bathroom, where they're not only embossed on the disposable towels, but hand-painted on the toilet seat covers and the tissue holders. The soap also rises with the carved manes of horse's heads. I get out fast when I start conjuring up scenes from *The Godfather*, which, considering my recent speculations, really creeps me out.

Since I had to separate from Kevin to use the bathroom, my plan to slip into the meeting under the cover of his company isn't working. Freddie, in character with the surroundings, cuts me off at the pass.

"What are you doing here, Ruby?"

"Nice to see you, too, Fred. You don't mind my being here, do you?"

"As long as you realize we have a reunion to finish up. And since the purpose is to perpetuate my family history, I'm continuing to take a leadership role."

"Essie Sue couldn't have said it better," I say, apparently thoroughly confusing him. "And by the way," I add, "I just came along with the rabbi to see if I could help."

I'd like to say a lot more, but I'd just as soon stay under his radar. Although anyone who could assume that the purpose of this reunion was merely to perpetuate his family history obviously doesn't send out radar — he's in his own orbit.

"You're always welcome here, Ruby. My husband forgets his manners once in a while, but you're one of his favorite people."

Now I see what Francie does — she smoothes out the wrinkles. She throws an arm around me and leads me into the living room where we're meeting — a cavernous space where enormous paintings of, yep, horses are hung on dark, wood-paneled walls.

The truth is, I have a *thing* for horses, in moderation. I even like some Western bronzes, but in this house I feel I'm lost on the set of *Giant*. Like those Fort Worth art collections where the canvases were commissioned by the yard, the Fenstermeister abode can only be described by the words *big* and *more*. And horses aren't the only things memorialized here — these people worship consumption in all its forms.

Francie seems dwarfed by her surroundings, and I doubt that as the second wife she selected even one piece of the furniture. Freddie's overbearing mother, an heir to the original hat factory fortune, was responsible for most of it, and the quest was continued every year abroad by Freddie's first wife, June, who inhaled collectibles everywhere from the Far East to the Home Shopping Network.

June also continued her mother-in-law's tradition of picking out all of Freddie's clothes and even feeding him from buffet tables at parties — she'd reach up and put the food right in his mouth — or take it out of his hands if it was something he wasn't supposed to eat. Freddie was pretty much overwhelmed by both women, but he broke free courtesy of his midlife crisis to marry one of his cashiers — Francie. Since she was the one woman in his life who called him *boss,* she was the perfect fit.

Freddie's starting the meeting with more scheduling, which definitely doesn't interest me. I'm sitting in back of the room on one of the twin carved stools June found in Thailand. I can slip away whenever I want without being noticed, but first I'm making sure that the glass display case with the Fabergé eggs is still in the living room. It's here, and just as Francie said to Clementine, there's only one egg. It's a blue one.

This seems like a good time to fade out. I'd like to come back for the conversation after the meeting, just to see how Fred handles the subject of Max Cole if someone brings it up. So far, none of the people at this committee meeting know about Hal, but it's only a matter of time. Kevin promised he wouldn't say anything. Meanwhile, I'd love to poke around, especially in this altar to *Things* — there's so much stuff here I won't have any trouble disappearing in it.

I don't know what I expect to find on this sniffing trip — it's been so long since I was here that I don't even remember my way around the house. If I'm seen I can always say I was looking for a telephone. That's a joke in this age of cell phones, but it still works.

"Is that you, Mrs. Rothman?"

Beverly Thomas, the Fenstermeisters' cook, taps me on the shoulder and nearly gives me a heart attack. She used to work in the temple kitchen on a freelance basis before she landed this job — a much more lucrative one.

I recover in time to greet her like a normal person would. "I haven't seen you in ages," I say. "How's your family?"

"Come have some coffee with me," she says. "I have some great Brie and crusty bread I haven't served yet."

She obviously still remembers my weakness for Brie, and I accept the invitation. I'd love to be able to ask her some questions about the Fenstermeisters, but it's not exactly kosher to expect her to talk about her employers, so I won't. Maybe the subject will come up spontaneously.

"How's that boy of yours?" she says. "I remember him hanging around the temple kitchen on Fridays after school, to see if any good-looking cookies had been dropped off."

"Ha. He's the same, still waiting. But a lot bigger boy than you remember." I update her on Josh's life as an adult, and let her know about the new foundling he left me.

Beverly's kids are out of the nest, too, and this job helps keep them out. "I even have something left for myself once in a while," she says. "They treat me pretty good here."

"You don't have to clean, too, do you?"

She laughs at that one. "To dust off all those statues and —"

"We call them tchotchkes," I say.

"Whatever. They couldn't pay me enough to keep after all that. Some other poor soul does it, and she has a lot more patience than I do. Plus a steadier hand. There are a bunch of statues in the study, too — they're the real dust-collectors."

So it appears that Freddie's doing okay in this economy if he can hire two servants and maybe more. Which tells me nothing, really. We make more small talk while I enjoy the coffee and Brie and she prepares the trays for passing when the meeting's over. When I try to help, she refuses. But when she attempts to lift too many of the heavy silver platters at once, she slips on her way to the table.

"Hey, watch it," I say as she rights herself. "The job isn't worth ruining your back. How many more do you need?"

"Only a couple," she says, pointing to the lazy Susan–type shelving which neatly holds the large trays in place until they're needed, then swings them out for convenience. I'd love a kitchen like this — wonder if Oy Vey could fit herself between these big shelves and go along for the ride.

I look to see which two fancy platters I should choose, and I fully intend to take them out one at a time. I don't owe Freddie a bad back, either. There are five or six more on separate shelves, each more ornate than the other — no surprise in this atmosphere. Since Beverly's still filling the previous ones, I take my time and look at them. Nosey Parker, but hey, I accepted that part of myself a long time ago. The one on the bottom is heavy silver, too, but it's sleek in a Nordic sort of way. Maybe a gift, but definitely not something native to this household. Plus, I could swear I've seen it somewhere.

I take each of the two platters over to Beverly, who smiles thanks. I'm itching to ask her about the bottom platter and why it's different, but something holds me back. Even though she might give me some good information, I'd still be calling attention to it. Best to leave it where it is.

We say our good-byes and I remind her to holler if she needs any help at serving time. Both of us know she won't —

Francie wouldn't understand and now that I think of it, I don't need any attention brought to my little visit, anyway.

As I leave the kitchen I listen for the dull chatter and foot shuffling that will tell me the meeting has broken up. It's quiet. Maybe I can get a look at the statues in Freddie's study while they're still haranguing in the living room. Is it upstairs? Part of me's thinking I shouldn't press my luck after the successful visit with Beverly in the kitchen, but on the other hand, when will I get a chance to be in Freddie and Francie's house again?

I'm prepared with my cover story as I race up the Scarlett and Rhett staircase — red-carpeted just like theirs. I need some aspirin for a horrible headache, and I didn't want to disturb the meeting, so I'm headed upstairs to see if I can find their maid to give it to me. If I don't see the maid but happen to find myself near a bathroom, I'm hoping an aspirin bottle might be in plain view on the bathroom counter, since I'd certainly never open the medicine cabinet. That's good enough — not great, but okay. I won't have to make any excuse for not asking Beverly for the aspirin, because no one saw us and Beverly's not about to tell her boss she entertained me with coffee in the kitchen. This is not something that would be encouraged by these people.

There's a greater chance I could actually be caught inside the study. In that case, I'll say I'm looking for the bathroom. In this spacious abode, there's probably a bathroom off the study anyway.

I find a cover story is much more believable if I can live it for a few minutes, so I get into headache mode as I walk down the second-floor corridor. I don't find the bathroom, which is fine because I'm not supposed to, but I do find the study. It's not too far from the stairs in case I need a quick getaway.

As I walk in, I'm greeted by more livestock, although these are horses of a different color. Instead of bronze, the medium is wood — there must be twenty wood horse carvings here, obviously carefully collected. The man sure has a passion for amassing, with the money to back it up. I don't know how he gets any work done here — every square foot is covered with merchandise. The whole Office Depot catalog seems to be laid out on the gargantuan oak desk, and I'm practically tripping over the scanners, printers, copiers, computers, and faxes. I'm bending down to look at one of the lower shelves when I hear a rustle behind me.

I don't turn around, but immediately put both hands up to my temples and attempt something between a sigh and a groan. Then I slowly get up and lean forward against a file cabinet, rubbing my scalp and remaining deep in my private predicament. Still facing away from where I heard the rustle, I move one hand to take an exaggerated look at my watch.

"What the hell are you doing up here, Ruby?"

It's Freddie, standing in the doorway.

"Hoping to find some aspirin in this study," I say without missing a beat. This is where being into it counts.

"I came up here to look for your maid or at least to find a family bathroom where there might be an aspirin bottle out in the open. There wasn't anything in the guest bath downstairs."

Ha. I don't even have to pretend, because right on cue, my head starts throbbing. When I get a sudden headache, I usually lose color in my face, so that should help, too. I'll bet he can see I'm pale.

"You've never been short on chutzpah," he says.

"So can you help me out?" I say.

Somehow I don't relish the thought of having him close that massive study door with the two of us inside, so I ease past him and head out into the corridor, where I feel safer. I think I'm carrying this off pretty well, although I have no idea if he's buying it.

"I'll get Francie up here to get it," he says. "The maids are busy."

"Thanks," I say, sitting down on the top step of the staircase. I guess fetching things is women's work.

"Is the meeting over already?" I say. "Did it go all right?"

He doesn't answer me, and goes downstairs.

I have to admit that I didn't expect him to be upstairs the minute the meeting broke up — if it did break up. I figured he'd be too busy meeting and greeting. I guess I'm stuck here until he sends someone up, so I spend the time massaging my head. Francie soon appears, and I figure I have to talk the talk all over again — it's beginning to bore me. But I guess Freddie cued her in, because she extends a hand to help me up from the top stair and heads us toward the master bedroom.

"Sorry to take you away from your

guests," I say. "I was looking for one of the maids."

She could be assuring me I'm not a nuisance, but she isn't. In the bathroom she wordlessly brings out the Bayer bottle, and I swallow three of them with the water she pours me.

"Thanks again, Francie," I say. "Maybe some coffee with caffeine will help."

She nods, but that's the most I can get out of her. She seems preoccupied.

When we get downstairs I head for where the coffee's set up. I'm suddenly hungry, too, and wolf down a half piece of coffee cake while I'm looking for the guy who brung me.

"Did Freddie say anything about Max Cole's murder when he talked to the group?" I whisper in Kevin's ear as soon as I find him.

"No, he talked about what we're doing the rest of the reunion and how he wants the committee to make this a memorable event for all the out-of-town guests."

I'm incredulous. "He doesn't think it'll be memorable enough as it is with someone getting murdered? Who'll ever forget it?"

As usual, my observations are totally lost on Kevin.

"You asked me what he said, and that's what he said."

He tries to pretend I'm not there, but I won't let him. Although I decide not to burden him with the events of the past fifteen minutes, I do pull him aside as everyone's noshing. I need to forget about my close call in the study and get back to what happened in the kitchen.

"Kevin, when you were photographing the liver mold for Essie Sue, do you remember what the platter looked like?"

I know what the answer's going to be, but I have to start somewhere.

"What do you mean *what the platter looked like?*"

"I mean would you recognize it if you saw it again?"

"No. It was just a silver platter. Like those."

"Are you sure it's like those?"

"Yeah. A platter. The one that disappeared after the murder. Look, Ruby, I was much more interested in scooping up a bite of liver with a cracker than I was noticing what was holding it."

Of course he was, and I'm stupid for not realizing that when it comes to identifying that platter, I have a much better witness than Kevin. The police have photos of it.

"Can I get some more food now?" he says. "I didn't have much for dinner."

"Okay, but do me a favor and forget this conversation."

"I hate to tell you this, Ruby, but I figured out a long time ago I'd be better off forgetting most of our conversations. They only get me in trouble."

Not dumb, this man, despite giving that appearance.

I wait around until Kevin's ready to leave, which is as soon as he's finished his current plate. We're both wordlessly avoiding our host. For my part, I want to leave before he finds out about Hal and starts asking me questions. And I certainly don't want to make any more of the looking-for-aspirin story than I already have. Kevin, as always, is dodging any further assignments, period. We're about to escape unnoticed and unscathed when Freddie calls out to us.

"You're leaving without saying good-bye?" he says.

"You looked busy," I say, "and I'm still coping with a killer of a headache. We weren't being impolite — your hospitality, as always, was wonderful."

Freddie brightens up for a minute at the compliment and we're about to make an excellent exit, when Kevin insists on having the last word.

"We were rushing out without saying good-bye," he says, "because Ruby's been tired." I guess he didn't hear I already used the headache excuse.

"Ruby hasn't been getting sleep at night because they think she has sleep apnea," Kevin says. "She's taking a test for it tomorrow night. And besides that, she's been working on this Max Cole murder — she's helping the police like she always does. Max Cole might have been some kind of crook."

Just what Freddie needs to hear, but he keeps his cool.

"Yeah, yeah, I know all about sleep apnea," he says. "I took the test here, too, and I didn't have it. So Francie's stuck with my snoring."

"It's about interrupted breathing," I say. "You can snore without having sleep apnea." Which is what he just said, but I still feel the need to explain. The truth is I'm furious that Kevin even brought it up. I'm not exactly dying to have Freddie informed of my sleeping habits.

16

E-mail from: Ruby
To: Nan
Subject: *Three in the Morning and I Still Can't Sleep*

Sorry I could only leave that cryptic message on your answering machine earlier with the news about Hal Margolis. Hal's no killer, Nan — Paul's known him for years, and he ought to go with his gut on this one. I thought I was in Wonderland last night when he called us into Kevin's study after services and marched Hal off to Austin for questioning.

When I got home I had a message from Essie Sue — she wanted my advice on contacting an attorney — just in case. We settled on Mark Franklin's brother Bill, who's based in Austin and has a good rep as a criminal lawyer. Essie Sue already has the room at the hotel, so staying in Austin is no problem. In fact, she was surrounded by mystery writers who'd been buzzing about little else since this man Max Cole was killed.

I had quite an experience at the Fenstermeisters after Temple, but can't deal with telling you about it now.

More later . . .

E-mail from: Nan
To: Ruby
Subject: *Oy*

Glad Essie Sue has the mystery writers for support — maybe she should hire one of them!

I'm assuming this is it for the Temple Rita reunion, huh? With its chief of operations out of commission, there won't be much incentive to continue, I guess.

What's Josh doing now that you're so preoccupied? And is poor Oy Vey's nose any better?

E-mail from: Ruby
To: Nan
Subject: *More*

Oy Vey's nose is better, but still out of

joint over his new roomie. The little orange guy is cute and is getting to me, but he's the last thing I needed to complicate my life right now. I'll have to deal with it, though, because Joshie's leaving tonight. He doesn't want to risk turning off his new colleagues in systems design before they can get through the first few weeks of break-in time. I'm getting a kick out of his following in my footsteps — although my freelance work developing small business systems bears no resemblance to Joshie's more complicated job.

And you're wrong — the reunion is not off. This very afternoon, the reunioners are spending free time with their Eternal hosts and preparing to bus back to Austin tonight for an art exhibit. Essie Sue also insists that since the big banquet Sunday night is already paid for, the show must go on.

My personal opinion is that Essie Sue's in denial, and is working overtime on this event to convince herself and everyone else that this interest in Hal is just a blip on the Margolis radar. I'm all for being upbeat, but she's told herself the whole thing's a fluke, and a trivial one at that. First of all, none of this is trivial — it's going to take that good lawyer for Hal to negotiate his way through the process. We still know nothing about the victim, other than that he's a small-time crook, or has been in the past. Hal denies knowing him.

It's not surprising that Hal's fingerprints are on the brass pestle if he brought it to the hotel, but his are the only ones, apparently. Of course, the real killer could have worn gloves. Paul's going to fill me in as soon as he's able.

P.S. I'm wearing that new black dress to the banquet on Sunday night.

E-mail from: Nan
To: Ruby
Subject: *Say That Again?*

Hey, you threw that at me pretty fast. Did you just say you were wearing that sexy dress you bought last month on sale? To *this* event? What gives?

E-mail from: Ruby
To: Nan
Subject: *Why Not?*

Just FYI, I asked Paul if he'd like to come up to the banquet with me. It's not a date.

E-mail from: Nan
To: Ruby
Subject: *??*

What Is It, Then?

17

Milt pours his special Kenya for me — black and hot. Joshie takes a double latte, and Kevin has tea — Good Seasons Original. We've already dug into a big late lunch platter of assorted bagels, hot from the oven. Mine's pumpernickel. It's mid-afternoon, and Milt has laid out egg salad scoops, lox, several flavors of cream cheese, and sliced tomatoes and green peppers to top our bagels. We're having navel oranges and fresh baked rugalach with cinnamon and raisins for dessert if we have any room left.

Joshie's the guest of honor, since he's leaving tonight and hasn't been to The Hot Bagel during his visit. I'm determined to spend time with him before he goes, so I'm saving any meetings with Paul until tomorrow. Paul's not going to think much of that silver platter I found, anyway, unless I have more to back it up. Today I have enough to do getting Josh off and preparing for the sleep apnea test tonight.

I wish I could say our talk here at lunch was as jolly as the occasion, but it's not — we're all obsessed with Hal's questioning and with speculation about the murder. I could turn the conversation in a brighter direction, but I'm in terrier-dog mode. I decided to pin Kevin down about every move he made when he was helping Essie Sue and Hal get ready for the reception the night of the murder. He's the only one who was with them — at least the only one I know about — and I need to establish a chronology. At this point there are too many missing pieces — I can't even speculate as to what might have happened.

"What did you do, Kevin?"

"Whaddaya mean, what did I do? I was on the setup crew, and I did whatever Essie Sue told me."

"No, I'm talking specifically about Thursday afternoon when we drove to the hotel together. We were early. You were supposed to go help with the reception preparations, and I stayed in the cocktail lounge — people-watching some of the KillerCon crowd. Then you came into the bar about an hour later and asked me to take you to Dr. Pascal's office."

"Yeah, I told the police where we were already. They wrote it down. And I gave them the dentist's address and phone number."

"I'm more interested in the hour I

wasn't with you, Kevin. Did you help them arrange the table, or schlepp things, or what? And who did it with you?"

"Lieutenant Lundy asked me all that, too, Ruby. Essie Sue and Hal were busy carrying stuff from the parking garage to their hotel suite. They were in a hurry because the reception was scheduled to begin soon, and they didn't have everything done. They gave me their digital camera and asked me to go to the party room we were using and take some photos of Essie Sue's Texas chopped liver mold that was already on ice. She wanted the pictures for the temple archives."

History in the making. Not that this is any big surprise — someone told me Essie Sue has her copperized baby shoes in the temple archives, too.

"Oh, and Ruby, Essie Sue already gave the camera to the police, and they downloaded the photos. So I can prove that."

"I know that, Kevin. I'm not grilling you because you did anything wrong. I simply want to know."

"But you grill worse than they do."

This observation gets a grin from my only son, who's survived being a grillee himself more than a few times.

Kevin's still fidgeting as if he has to

prove something, so I let up, and stuff my mouth with a great big orange section. It's not that I don't know I can be a pest when I'm in this mode. And I guess I'm extra sensitive because Josh is here. Childhood memories are one thing, but I'm not dying to remind him of all my frailties when I don't even see him that often. I'd like to at least give him the *chance* to think I've improved with age. Yeah, right. As if our kids aren't clued in to the whole catalog of our imperfections.

To my surprise, Milt, who's been listening abstractedly while supplying us with fresh coffee, suddenly picks up where I left off, and starts questioning Kevin himself.

"Rabbi, I'd think you'd feel relieved that you told the police everything. How come you look so nervous every time we talk about any of this?"

I hadn't been consciously aware of it, but Kevin has been awfully jumpy about that afternoon.

"Don't forget, Milt," Josh says, taking up for him, "he had that whole broken tooth incident. That wasn't exactly a pleasant memory."

"Is that what it is, Rabbi?" Milt says.

"Probably," Kevin says. "The whole thing, you know?"

"I know it's upsetting," Milt says. "But there's no police here — just us. Did you see anyone, or can you think of anything else that might have happened while you were taking those photos?"

Kevin takes a big bite of his second bagel and cream cheese, chews it, and follows up with a swig from his mug of tea. He wipes his mouth with a napkin and sits at attention — or as close to attention as he's capable of.

"No one was there," he says. "And there was nothing else relevant to the murder that happened during that time."

We all perk up. I can hardly keep my mouth shut, but since the others at the table are every bit as effective as I've been at interrogating Kevin, I wait to see their reactions. The funny thing is that Essie Sue's the one person who'd end this hesitancy if anyone could — he'd undoubtedly spill it all to her.

"Is this something you'd rather tell Essie Sue?" I say.

Kevin's skin looks as pale yellow as the egg salad. He slides his chair from the table, apparently ready to make a run for it.

"Essie Sue's the last person I want to talk to about this," he says as he throws his napkin on the table.

"Come on, Rabbi," Milt says, putting his big arm around Kevin and giving him a noodge to stay seated. "Maybe we can help you feel better. Just tell us what's on your mind." This and a fresh rugalach on his plate seem to stay the flight response.

"Ruby already knows about it," he says.

"Huh? I do?"

Everyone looks at me, but I have absolutely no clue.

"Is this something you told me and I've forgotten?" I ask.

"You and Dr. Pascal," Kevin says.

"We both know? I have no idea what you're talking about."

"Well, you know the important part. The only relevant part," he says.

My impatience is overcoming my curiosity now, and I forget to be polite to Kevin.

"Come on, Kevin, out with it. You fractured the tooth and I took you to the dentist — end of story as I know it. Quit pussyfooting."

I guess I remind him of Essie Sue, so he cracks.

"Well, the only thing I did other than take the photos while I was there was to try a little of the chopped liver. Essie Sue'll kill me if she finds out. She told me not to dare touch her masterpiece — just to photograph it. She even made me promise to wear my camera around my neck so it wouldn't drop accidentally on the State of Texas."

"We won't tell her," Milt says. "Give us the details."

"Okay, I went to the reception room. It was early and everything was already set up — Essie Sue and Hal had put the mold on ice, and the crackers and other stuff were already out — the only things left to go were the hot appetizers, and they were being saved for the waiters to bring at the last minute.

"The light was good, and I took the close-ups from every angle — Essie Sue's pretty demanding about that. I've taken pictures of her tables before."

"That sounds pretty relevant to me, Rabbi," Joshie says. "So what did you do there that you felt *wasn't* relevant?"

It looks like all three of us are hooked now, even my son, who's trying to bring logic into the mix.

"It was really nobody's business, Josh," Kevin says. "I was all alone, and I just got kind of hungry. What's the matter with that?"

We all shrug, hoping we convey enough sympathy to make Kevin feel he'd done absolutely nothing wrong in having a little forbidden snack and risking Essie Sue's wrath. Meanwhile, we're all in awe that he dared to do it.

"You've got to admit, her liver is spectacular," Kevin says. "It smelled delicious."

"And it's a big state," I say.

"Right, Ruby. I thought to myself that she'd be too busy to notice if I used a cracker to excavate a bite and then filled up the hole afterward. So I dug in."

"Around Fort Worth?" I ask, hoping that specifics will keep him focused.

"No, actually, I kind of honed in on Austin," he says. "It felt familiar."

"So?" Milt looks goggle-eyed at this point.

"So that's when I bit down on a shell from a nut or a chicken liver bone or something and broke my tooth."

Milt and I look at each other. Not even Essie Sue puts nuts in chopped liver, and chicken livers don't have bones. But no one wants to contradict Kevin.

"What did you do?" I ask.

"I got scared and ran out of the room before someone could see I'd been eating. Luckily, no one saw me."

"That's when you found me in the cocktail lounge," I say.

"Yeah. Then we went to the dentist and I got away with sneaking that bite, except for the pain. I think of that broken tooth as payback, you know?"

"I don't understand what you meant when you said Dr. Pascal and I knew all about it. All about what? That you bit down on something?"

"Dr. Pascal didn't even want to see it. But when I gave it to you, you might have noticed that I bit down on something that could be associated with the liver. I'm talking about the piece of nut I gave you wrapped up in the cocktail napkin."

I mentally smack myself up the side of the head as I vaguely recall Kevin handing me something.

"I didn't associate anything with anything, Kevin. And if I had, so what? I wasn't going to rat you out to Essie Sue."

"Well, I can't say I worried about that, but it's just something I wanted to keep secret when the police questioned me."

"I know — it wasn't relevant," I say.

"It was something that happened at the murder scene," Josh says. "I'd say that might be important. Did you throw the napkin away, Mom?"

"I have no idea. Kevin was bleeding and hurting. My main interest was in driving him to the dentist."

"You put it in your coat pocket," Kevin says. "I remember being surprised Dr. Pascal didn't ask you for it, but I guess he was in too much of a hurry."

"We all were," I say. "It was the end of the workday for them, and you and I were due at the reception. I never gave it another thought."

Josh reaches around to the next table, where I've thrown my coat.

"Same coat?" he says.

"I think so."

He reaches deep into the pocket and brings out — yep, a wadded-up napkin. We're all pretty intent on what's a fairly gross object as Josh unfurls the paper. The napkin does indeed contain something covered in blood and brownish dried liver, but it doesn't look like any nut or bone *I've* ever seen.

When Joshie wipes the tiny fragment with the napkin, he uncovers something man-made. It's a square metal object the size of a postage stamp.

"This is what you bit down on, Rabbi," he says.

"What in the world is that?" Kevin asks him.

"It's a piece of flash memory."

"You mean like a computer chip?" Milt says.

"One thing's for sure," I quip in vain to a totally unresponsive audience, "it ain't chopped liver."

18

Josh and I get out of there as soon as possible, because we're both aware that he'll be flying home in only a few hours. I know him well — after all, he's got my genes — and he's no doubt already figuring how long we'll have on the computer before he has to pack his suitcase. A friend he hasn't seen yet is taking him to the airport tonight since I have to take that sleep test, and they can have a short visit in late afternoon.

"The rabbi's a pretty conventional guy," he says, "so I'm really surprised he didn't feel obligated to tell the cops everything that happened on the scene that afternoon."

"Oh, he was probably worried about abbreviating his story for Paul Lundy," I say, "but to Kevin, the consequences of that would pale beside having to tell Essie Sue that he profaned the sacred centerpiece. You have no idea what a hold she has over him."

"So how come you and Dad lasted so long under the intimidation?"

"We were different people, that's all; we

had each other, and what's the worst she could do to us? Kevin's insecure about getting another job — I think he really likes it here."

"It wouldn't be worth it to me," he says. "I hate kowtowing to anyone."

"Look, Joshie, I don't care how independent you are or think you are, your work has to please someone. You can call yourself a freelancer or a consultant or whatever, but other people have to buy your product or accept your advice or want to support your efforts. Everyone has a boss, even if that boss is just the general public."

He doesn't have an answer, which usually means he can see my point but has to think about it. When he disagrees, like me — he never keeps it a secret.

"I wonder what Hal had to do with Max Cole," Josh says as we pull into our driveway.

"He says he had nothing to do with him," I say. "And since Essie Sue was asking everyone who Max was, I'm convinced she didn't know him. Can you imagine Hal knowing someone who was unknown to Essie Sue?"

"Yes, I could. People like Essie Sue are exactly the kind others won't confide in —

even their spouses. Especially their spouses. And look at the rabbi — he edited his police statement because of her."

"Maybe this computer chip will tell us something. It's Secure Digital memory, isn't it? That seems to be one of the tiniest, and this thing is certainly small."

"Your computer has a card reader that can read any of these brands, Mom, which is a break for us."

"I know — I don't use those Secure Digital chips, so ordinarily, we'd have to have it read by someone else. I'm glad my reader has the flexibility."

"I'd be surprised if it didn't. You have everything else up-to-date."

"I am in the business, not that I've made much money at it lately."

We take a peek at Oy Vey and Chutzpah, who, to our surprise, have been curled up together on the back porch. They spring apart when they hear us. Oy Vey gives a weak snort, and Chutzpah waves a paw at him, no doubt to let us know that what we saw wasn't for real. I'm beginning to get the picture here, and I'm a lot less worried about the two of them killing each other than I was a few days ago.

"Do you think you should get your clothes ready first?" I say.

"No. Let's go to your office."

He's got the wadded-up napkin in his own shirt pocket, so I can't protest too much. Besides, I really want him here in case I have a problem with the reader not working. This isn't the time to go running off for help and have to spread the word. Neither of us mentions the fact that, like Kevin, we're also keeping information to ourselves that the police would dearly love to see. I promised Milt and Kevin that I'd report back to them ASAP, and of course at some point soon I have to let Paul in on all this.

Oy. Just as I'm about to sit down at the computer, the phone rings and I pick it up automatically. I hate myself when I do this — having caller ID has never seemed to stop me from grabbing the phone the way I always do — the downside of low impulse control. Joshie glares at me and looks at his watch, but it's too late.

"Hi, honey. I've been thinking about you and wanted to check in."

It's of course my ever-lovin' and ESP-attuned guy on the phone from San Antonio, who's calling to see what's happened since yesterday.

I give a quick shrug to Josh and point to his bedroom where the suitcase is, but he doesn't pick up the hint. He waits.

"Hi, babe. Josh has to leave soon, so I might have to call you back, okay?"

"Don't hang up *that* fast — can't you talk for a minute? I was thinking I'd come up tomorrow and go to the final reunion banquet with you. How do you feel about it?"

Now he wants to come.

"I'd like that, Ed. But I did ask Paul to go along, too, since I had the extra ticket and you weren't coming."

Silence on the other end.

"Okay, I guess that's only fair," he says finally. "They'll sell me another ticket, won't they?"

"The ticket's not a problem. If you're coming, you can use it. I'm sure they'll let Paul in without one, since he's police."

"So this is professional with him?"

I look at Joshie, but he isn't budging, so I signal I won't stay on long.

"Ed, if you're asking me whether Paul was planning to be at the dinner anyway, the answer is *no* — I invited him. What he does when he gets there is up to him, and I'm sure, with all that's happened, he'll be wearing two hats."

"That's what I've been trying to figure out, Ruby — what's his other hat here?"

"Are you jealous?"

"Maybe. I know he's interested in you. I just don't know what's up on your end."

This is the last place I want to be having this conversation. I've already said more than I should have with Josh here, and time's running out before we need to leave.

"Ed, I really want to see you tomorrow. But I'm on a deadline with Josh, and we'll have to talk about it when I see you. You're definitely coming up?"

"Definitely. Tell Josh good-bye for me."

Ed's voice sounds better already — I guess it's no secret I still want to see him. We ring off and Josh takes the phone off the hook while swiveling me around to face the computer. I find the memory card reader, which I don't use all that often. I connect it to the computer's USB port, slip the Secure Digital card into its slot, and click on the screen icon that pops up. It works.

What comes up on the screen has us in turn puzzled, astonished, and even more curious. The document, though brief, contains three sections.

Part One consists of detailed driving directions to a rest stop several miles from Austin, on a road leading west to the Hill Country. It specifies that the first of a series of payments be made in cash to be left at the rest stop at a certain time and place. There's no greeting or salutation to indicate who's involved.

Part Two lists the code for a Swiss bank account number where further payments are to be entered electronically upon receipt of an *Object* to be deposited in the bank's vaults.

Part Three consists of four color graphics — highly detailed, dense resolution digital photographs of a single blue Fabergé egg taken from four angles: top, underside, front, and back positions. An accompanying certificate beneath each photograph describes authenticating marks or signatures.

Josh looks at me. "This memory card is what the rabbi broke his tooth on?"

"We're lucky his tooth didn't break *this*," I say.

"It's not fair," Josh says. "I endure this whole reunion weekend, and just when things get interesting, I have to leave."

My kitchen timer goes off as an addendum to his words.

"I set the oven timer in case we got too wrapped up in this," I say.

"It wouldn't be the first time we lost all track of the clock," he says. "So that's all?

We can't even take that cocktail hour apart minute by minute?"

I feel as though I'm conversing with myself — that's why I always hate to see this kid go. But there's not a thing I can do about it now. He still has to throw his stuff into his duffel and say good-bye to Chutzpah.

"Let's do our speculating while you pack," I say.

19

E-mail from: Ruby
To: Nan
Subject: *Choices*

I'm telling you, Nan — you now know as much as I do. I faxed you the entire contents of the memory card, and the information there could have dropped from another planet for all I know. The card hidden in the liver could be connected in many ways, and of course Max Cole was also found dead in the same platter. This is why I'm so sorry Joshie had to leave earlier — he could have batted this around a bit more with me. Not that you aren't a good sounding board, too — it's just that you aren't *here*. Although that's never stopped us before — ha.

And yes, of course I have some hunches — what else is new? But they're off-the-wall at this point. I'll tell you about them in another note, but right now, my problem isn't my speculations, it's whom to confide in. Okay, Paul is the logical one, but he's so official. I know I'll have to tell him really soon, now that this new lead has developed. *Whenever* I inform him, he'll be obligated to pass the information along to his colleagues in Austin, since it's their case. Once that's done, all kinds of people will know.

Ed's not a good choice, either. He's chained to the newspaper, and although I'd love to rely on him later on, I can't ask him to promise me not to use this information. Plus, how would it look to Paul if Ed knew before he did?

I certainly owe Milt and Kevin a call — they've been involved since noon, and are waiting to hear. But Kevin's sometimes a loose cannon. Then there's Hal and his lawyer, who have a need to know, not to mention *you-know-who.*

Waddaya think? I'm glad tomorrow's Sunday and you don't have to go to work. By the way, I'll give you a full report, by phone or e-mail, on the sleep apnea test I scheduled for tonight.

E-mail from: Nan
To: Ruby
Subject: *I'm Here*

Sorry Josh isn't there, babe — he's a doll.

Okay, answers. You need to call the rabbi and Milt — just to be a mensch, of course, but that doesn't mean you can't wait a bit. Knowing you, you'll use your caller ID to keep them at bay. Unless you feel Milt can help you think — in that case, contact him now. I'm guessing, though, that if he could fill your requirements, you'd already be on the phone with him.

You know I'm very partial to Paul — I admire his reasoning. My feedback would be to get him over to your house ASAP, but to tell him candidly that although you realize his obligation to pass along any information you're giving him, you're pleading for a couple of hours to bat around your ideas with him before he goes on the record.

We both also know that you don't *have* many ideas yet, but that's never stopped you. You work well with him, and I'll bet he'll *want* to brainstorm with you. Legally, you can't leave him out of the loop for long, and you can also use him as an excuse to hold off the rabbi and Milt if you have to.

Let me know how it goes and what you decide. If you're too busy today with so little time before your test, I can wait.

E-mail from: Ruby
To: Nan
Subject: *Hugs*

This is why I pay you so much . . . ha! Your advice couldn't be better.

Stay tuned.

20

Of all the scenarios I'd pictured, leaving a message for Paul at the station, on his cell, and at home, wasn't on my list. Now I'm left wondering: (a) where he is on a sunny Saturday afternoon, (b) why do I care, and (c) is he going to have time to listen to me? This could be an advantage, though — he might feel less pressure to do any reporting about this in the middle of the weekend.

I try to still my churning insides by checking on the animals — I promised Joshie not to zone out on what he calls their relationship. I head into the breakfast room, Chutzpah's favorite hangout — it didn't take him long to make himself at home on the rug under the table. Since I knew Oy Vey would follow me, I now have a chance to see firsthand if the bonding is holding up as well as it did when Josh was here.

It's not. Chutzpah hisses the minute he sees Oy Vey, who retaliates with a low growl. I'm glad to see my dog's at least standing up to the interloper. I guess I'm giving myself away here, and I'm glad Josh is not around to sense it. I'm feeling sorry for Oy Vey — she never bargained for this. Neither did I, although it's not Chutzpah's fault that I couldn't stand up to my own flesh and blood. I *could* have sent the cat back, after all.

Guilty, I sit down on the floor and try to coax both of them into my lap or at least in the vicinity. To my surprise, they come. Oy Vey lies with her head in my lap, while Chutzpah jumps into whatever space is left — not much. I'm petting one of them with each hand and explaining the principles of coexistence in a way I wouldn't want a living soul to overhear, when the phone rings. I grab it to look at the caller ID in case it's anyone but Paul. It's him.

"Just a minute, Paul," I say, "let me get to the other room."

I suddenly realize I've alarmed him.

"I'm okay," I say. "This isn't an emergency." No, he'll think it *is* one — why else would I be calling three of his phones? "Well, it is an emergency of sorts, but I'm fine — just hold on, okay?"

I dump the disappointed pair from my lap as politely as I can, and run to my office, where Oy Vey promptly follows. Chutzpah, I notice as I leave, turns his back.

"I'm here, Paul."

"Yeah, I can figure that out." He sounds put off — maybe he's on an afternoon date. "So since this isn't a real emergency, what gives, Ruby?"

"First, what are you doing right now? If you're out with someone, this will wait until tomorrow — just tell me. But if you're not, I need you to come over here. I know it sounds weird, but you've got to trust me on this one, Paul."

"I just got home, Ruby, and I can come over if you need me. But can't you say anything more on the phone?"

"Believe it or not, I can't. Only that this is something concerning the case, and I don't think you'd want me to hold off telling you."

"I'm on my way."

"I'll put on a pot of coffee."

I feel a sense of relief just being able to unload this on Paul. I make extra-strong coffee for us and warm up some blackberry cobbler I threw together for Josh — it's not bad, either. I've got Bluebell Homemade Vanilla ice cream if he wants it on top.

I'll bet he *has* been out on an afternoon date — when he pulls up in the driveway and gets out of the car, he's wearing the kind of sport clothes he'd save for something special — a black turtlenecked sweater, khakis, and nice loafers. I'm used to seeing him in jeans and sweats when he's off work, and I can't help looking twice at the way that sweater shows off his muscular frame.

I give him a quick hug and bring him in the house before my nosy neighbor across the street sticks her head out the window. "You look good" is all I say. I'm proud of myself for keeping my mouth shut about the date possibility — it's none of my business. Not that that's stopped me before.

I pour him a mug of coffee and put the ice cream carton on the kitchen table before I sit down with him, so I won't be distracted. He hates it when I don't get to the point, and I'm determined not to keep him waiting.

"Josh and I were at The Hot Bagel today with Rabbi Kevin and Milt," I say. "Remember when Kevin told you about our trip to the dentist making us late to the reception? And how he bit down on a nut and broke his tooth?"

"Yeah, I was trying to get him to account for the time he spent away from you when you were in the cocktail lounge. He said he was taking pictures for Essie Sue."

154

"And after he took the pictures, it seems that he sampled some of Essie Sue's chopped liver mold," I say. "He left some things out of his account to the police."

I can see Paul visibly setting his jaw. He puts down the forkful of cobbler he was about to eat.

"It's just Kevin," I say, "he didn't mean anything by it. He was afraid Essie Sue would be angry with him, and he didn't think leaving that part out would make any difference."

"So what *did* he leave out?"

"Kevin bit down on something hard when he tasted the chopped liver. He thought it was a nut, and when his tooth bled, he saved part of the tooth and the nut in a paper napkin. Apparently, he told me to put it in my coat pocket until I could give it to the dentist for him. The dentist didn't want to see it then, and I forgot about it until he reminded me this afternoon."

"Doesn't sound very relevant to me, either, Ruby."

"That's what I thought. But when I opened the napkin he'd asked me to keep, the hard thing he bit down on turned out not to be a nut."

I take a swig of coffee before I go on.

"You're not going to believe this," I say.

"Try me."

"It was a small chip of flash memory — a tiny Secure Digital card. Josh and I brought it home and loaded it onto my computer screen."

Paul's way ahead of me already. "So you're saying the victim, Max Cole, was killed in front of a platter — a missing platter — that at one time contained a computer chip?"

"Well, yes, I guess you could put it that way. Cole was found with his head in the ice bed that once held Essie Sue's chopped liver mold. We know the mold was there because Kevin took pictures of it, and because he now says he ate some of it."

"So Cole could have been looking for it."

"Yep. But you haven't heard the best part."

"Don't be cute, Ruby — just tell me. Did you make a printout?"

I hand him the chip and the pages I've printed. "These wouldn't have meant much to you if I hadn't given you the context," I remind him.

"I know. Sorry. There's a lot to absorb here, and you know I'm not the most patient guy around."

Paul's the only person I know who reads as fast as I do — an occupational advantage, I'm sure. He gobbles the pages with his eyes in about ten seconds flat.

"Who knows about this?" he says.

"Joshie and me. But Josh's visit is over."

"You didn't tell the rabbi and Milt yet?"

"No. I thought I'd better let you see it first."

He reads the printout again. "Just so we're on the same page here, Ruby, what do you get from this? And I'm asking just to be clear — this stuff is stand-alone information? You had no inkling of it from any other source?"

"Nope. That's it, Paul. It just appeared on the Secure Digital card. What I get from it is that a valuable Fabergé egg was to be exchanged at a rest stop for some cash. And that more money was to be placed in a Swiss bank account when the egg was deposited in the bank's vault."

He pats my arm. "I like the way you think, Ruby. When you're not kidding around, you can be more concise than anyone I know. You're not giving me any speculation here, only a recitation of the facts."

"So when do we get to speculate?" I say.

He cracks a smile, but I can see his

whole face is animated, and not just from my question. I know from past experience that this is what he lives for.

"This is our first big break in this case," he says.

"So let's celebrate by eating some of the cobbler and taking our own break," I say.

We both relax in our chairs and chew silently. Oy Vey comes over to Paul to be petted. She likes him, but she also has an unbelievable sense of timing about these things — I know she waited, too, until there was a pause in our conversation.

Paul's absentmindedly rubbing Oy Vey's head with one hand and tapping on his coffee mug with the other. He's looking at the ceiling — something he does when he's concentrating hard.

"Maybe Max Cole was looking for that chip when he was killed," he says.

"But the whole platter was gone when the body was discovered," I say. "His head was in ice."

"His face had liver on it," Paul reminds me. "No, he was searching for that chip."

"Or putting it in there," I say.

"Nope — you're not thinking now, Ruby. Max was obviously there after the rabbi, not before. The rabbi took the chip, and then Max couldn't find it."

"Or maybe the killer couldn't find it," I say.

"Touché."

"So do you see Hal as the other person?" I say.

"I have no idea. But I certainly know more now about how to question him."

"The killer must have taken the liver mold," I say.

"Had to."

"Yeah, because he was still looking for that chip," I say, "and wanted time to find it."

"And the rabbi had it all the time. Unbelievable."

"I had it most of the time in my coat pocket."

We finish up our cobbler in silence. It's one of those moments I know I'll look back on — us, sitting around the table, excited and subdued at the same time, our minds working furiously and in sync.

"I'll call Austin when I leave here," Paul says.

"Hal didn't do it," I say as he gets up to go. "One of the Fenstermeisters did."

Paul lifts his eyebrows. "Is this like 'Columbo'?" he says. "Where we know the killer? Or at least you do?"

"They collect Fabergé eggs," I say, ignoring his remarks. "They have for years. I've seen them. I just didn't think they were real."

Paul sits back down at the table and swigs from his cup of cold coffee.

"And that's it?" he says. "That's your evidence?"

"Better than yours," I say, "even though I have to admit it's a stretch right now. But nobody else I know had Fabergés — they're worth a fortune. I'm as sure Freddie and Francie are involved as I am that Hal is innocent. Of course, proving that will be the hard part."

I'm ready for the brush-off, but it doesn't come.

"Okay, tell me more."

I explain about the eggs I've seen at Francie and Freddie's through the years, and I tell him about the other night when Francie swore to Clementine she only had one egg.

"No one ever thought the contents of that chip would become public," I say, "and you have to agree with me that the connection is much too coincidental. Who else in this town would have a Fabergé egg?"

"It's quite a reach to go from collector to killer, Ruby. But I will say one thing — the

160

circumstances of this murder are too weird to have been planned. The whole scene yells *amateur,* so I certainly can't rule out the Fenstermeisters."

"But without more, you have nothing," I say.

"You know the drill. On the other hand, we have one more day when everyone's together."

"A day and a breakfast," I say. "The Hot Bagel's catering a breakfast Monday morning before the reunion people leave."

Paul's now drumming his fingers on the tablecloth — a surer sign he's with me than the studiously blank look on his face.

"We have all day tomorrow before the big Sunday banquet. Maybe we can come up with something," I say.

"Something?" he says. "I don't like the sound of that. You know we appreciate your input, Ruby, but I'm reporting to Austin — they're in charge."

"Which means they'll do what?"

"They'll be the ones to formulate a plan if there is one. I'll personally work on any connection to the Fenstermeisters, and I'll keep you posted. I don't want information leaking to them before we're ready to pursue it."

I can feel the hair on my scalp starting to

161

stand up — Paul's worked with me count-less times and I've never yet let him down. Plus, I've just given the police their only solid lead in this murder case — a lot, if you ask me. Fortunately, I catch myself be-fore I react in a way I'll be sorry for. I want to get Paul out of here before I have to promise not to talk to Kevin or Milt.

"Can I make some hotter coffee? This stuff's ice-cold."

I get up from the table and head toward the electronics section of my kitchen: the simple juicer, the enormous Champion cruncher/juicer, the George Foreman grill, the KitchenAid mixer, the Oster blender, the Italian espresso machine, the bread maker, the electric wok, the toaster, the Nesco oven, and of course the coffeepot, which grinds beans, too.

As I figured he would, Paul takes that as his cue to leave again. He looks relieved that I'm not asking to help research the Fenstermeister art collection.

"Anything else I can do, Paul?" I guess that's pushing it, but it's too late to take the words back. At least it might keep him from thinking of what I'm *not* supposed to do.

"You've done quite enough," he says, and surprises me by giving me a smile that starts from the corners of his mouth but doesn't grow because he thinks better of it. He just looks at me instead. I guess he did appreciate my help.

"Do we still have a date for the banquet?" he says on the way out.

"Sure."

Why do I feel, after he's left, that I've just been kissed?

21

It takes me fifteen whole minutes dawdling over my own cold coffee cup to remember I just lied to Paul. I was so thrown by his exit lines that I forgot all about the banquet date with Ed I just made, and I also told Paul that Josh was the only one who knew about the computer chip. Nan knows, too.

I can't believe I was so flustered I forgot about Ed's call. But now that I think of it, I didn't exactly tell Ed it was a date — I told him he could use Paul's banquet ticket because Paul would get in anyway.

I'd like to dwell on the way Paul looked at me before he left, but the more pressing issue at the moment is how to make the most of tomorrow. My gut tells me that it's not going to be that easy for Paul to pin down the Fabergé connection between Freddie and Max Cole, especially with Hal Margolis's fingerprints all over the murder weapon. But it might be possible to psych Freddie out.

I put everything in the sink and pick up the phone — that's it for the cleanup. Even Oy Vey looks surprised — I hate to leave a sink full of dishes, and usually fill the dishwasher no matter what.

I promised Kevin I'd let him know right away what we found on the chip, and I owe him that much. After all, he started this — in his own weird way. And if I don't see him now, I'll have no time before the sleep apnea test tonight. Luckily, I don't have to show up there until nine.

It takes Kevin five rings to answer the phone.

"I was taking a nap, Ruby."

"Sorry, Kevin — you said you wanted to know about the chip. I'm taking the apnea test later, and I thought you ought to be caught up before you see everyone at the ceremonial art event tonight."

"Can you tell me on the phone, Ruby? This is everybody's free time, and I need mine."

"I don't think that's a good idea — I can come over to your house if you want. I won't glance at anything, Kevin — I couldn't care less how your apartment looks."

"Good. It's a mess. You promise you won't notice?"

"Who do you think I am — Essie Sue? I've got other things on my mind. I'll be over in a few minutes."

I make it to Kevin's apartment building in under fifteen minutes — let's just say I'm glad Paul's not monitoring my speedometer. I can see Kevin sticking his head out the door twice before I even get out of the car.

"What's the matter?" I say as he whisks me through the front door. "Afraid your neighbors will think you're acting in a manner unbecoming to the clergy? It's not even late."

"I don't need the gossip," he says.

"Maybe it'll be good for your image, Kevin. You could use a little action."

"Cut it out, Ruby. Tell me what's going on."

He's wearing his pajama top and a pair of dress pants, which he obviously threw on in my honor. We make our way into his kitchen, an area which gives the word *compact* a bad name, and he takes a big pitcher out of the refrigerator. It's full of a blue liquid.

"What is this?" I ask as he pours the stuff into two plastic Texas Longhorn glasses.

"Kool-Aid. I usually end up with it the last week of the month before my paycheck comes. It's cheap."

"That I'm sure of, but I didn't think you

were that bad off. We're not paying you bubkes, are we?"

"I'm saving up for the sports car I told you about."

"That'll help the image. But I still wouldn't bring the babes back here for Kool-Aid," I say.

We pick our way through the gym equipment that still makes up the bulk of Kevin's living room furniture. It's left over from Essie Sue's last venture into the bodybuilding business, when she liquidated her Center for Bodily Movement and sold Kevin the leftovers for a song, or in his case, a hymn. I go for the reclining bike, which is really quite comfortable and my personal favorite. Kevin sits cross-legged on the trampoline.

"Let's get this over with fast, Ruby. What did you find?"

I show him another printout of the payment instructions for the Fabergé egg and fill him in on the rest, including my speculations. I can tell he's not as fascinated by this as I was — his eyes are glazing over.

"I can't do anything about Freddie," he says. "He can't stand me, anyway."

"I know you didn't finish your nap, Kevin, but you did say you wanted to know about this as soon as possible."

"Yeah, thanks, Ruby. But don't count on me — I'll be lucky if my job's still here after Essie Sue finds out what I did. I don't need the Fenstermeisters on my back, too. If you think they're connected, you figure it out. Just keep me out of it. What would Freddie have to do with a weirdo like Max Cole, anyway?"

"I don't know. But Essie Sue says Hal had nothing to do with him, and I believe her. I watched the Margolises react to the murder, and I could see by the shock on their faces that they were playing it straight."

"So you've got me finding the computer chip in the liver mold. A little while later, Max is dead with his face where that mold has been. That's all you know, right, Ruby?"

"Paul is tracking more about Max, and I want to explore any connection between him and Freddie."

"You don't think Fred Fenstermeister's a murderer, do you?"

"Who knows? Juggling the Margolises and the Fenstermeisters is killing me."

"You're not the only one. I'm sorry I even took those photos, Ruby. I wish I'd had no part in this."

"Who has them now, Kevin?"

"I think the police asked Essie Sue for the camera when they questioned her after the murder."

"They were close-ups, right?"

"As close as I could get."

"Okay, Kevin, then I'm off to the police station before my sleep test. Paul's working late tonight — I want to talk to him once more today."

22

I catch Paul at the station when not much is happening — we practically have the place to ourselves.

"The Austin police were very interested in the material on the computer chip," he says, "and they're analyzing it. We're trying to see what Hal's connection could be to the contents of the Secure Digital card. We have people checking the bank accounts, too."

"Well, it's my own opinion that aside from his fingerprints on the murder weapon, which the killer would have anticipated, you're not going to find any connection, Paul. I just don't see why the police think his fingerprints add up to murder."

"At least we have something with the chip now," he says. "I know you're impatient as usual, but you're just going to have to stow it and let the pros do their thing. The detectives were appreciative, though — they wanted me to tell you."

"That's nice, but I'm on another track now."

Paul brings me a Diet Coke from the machine and pours a cup of their lousy coffee for himself — he doesn't even bother to ask if I want some — we've been through this ritual too many times. I let him scrounge me some peanut butter crackers from the other machine since I haven't had time for supper.

I tell him about the visit last night with Freddie's maid Beverly, and manage to minimize the part about my snooping foray in Freddie's study. I'd just get a lecture about risk, and I've heard it all before. Besides, all I did was get a peek at the statuary.

"What I need to see is those photos Kevin took of the liver mold," I say. "He told me they were in the camera when he gave it back to Essie Sue after he finished his assignment."

"Yeah, we have them. Austin downloaded them and e-mailed them to me here," he says. "I had the lab blow them up. Not that they showed much — there was no one lurking in the wings, if that's what you mean. Didn't even find one of those photographic auras the police psychics look for."

"Funny," I say. "I'm not searching for auras. I want to see the platter the liver was

171

on. The one that was sitting on the bed of crushed ice."

He finds the file and spreads a bunch of color photos on the table in front of us. Kevin has done a good job. He made sure to take the photos before he had his snack from the mold, and it lies gleaming on its ice bed. All the state's major cities and rivers are outlined in yellow cream cheese squeezed from an icing bag — a perfect example of cake decorating gone mad. I wouldn't say the brown liverish background is exactly appetizing, but who knows if Essie Sue would have let anyone touch it anyway.

Reflecting Kevin's zeal for close-ups, most of the photos feature the liver and not extraneous details like the platter and its accompanying tray of crushed ice. He's focused in tight on his subject. On one of the pictures, though, he seems to have stepped back a bit. At the very bottom of the photo, he's captured the silver platter.

"See — it's here," I tell Paul. "A further enlargement and you'll be able to tell for sure, but I can make out now that it's the same platter I saw in Freddie's kitchen — put away neatly on the very bottom of the shelf. It's sleek — like the Danish modern that was so popular in the fifties — with no froufrou like the Fenstermeisters' fancy trays."

"It's far out, Ruby," Paul says. He makes a face at his sour coffee, but keeps drinking it. "Too far out at this point."

"You mean because there are lots of platters like it, blah blah blah?"

"Plus the fact that we may not be able to pull up many additional features even when we blow it up again."

"What if you *can* identify it as being the same one that's in that kitchen, and then Beverly Thomas swears to you that she never saw a platter like that in their house before? She's worked there for several years, and they entertain a lot. She'd know."

"At least you didn't color her testimony by asking her already," he says. "You didn't, did you?"

I give him a stare and don't answer — he doesn't deserve one.

"I think putting it in with their own platters is the ideal hiding place," I say. "Rather than have it discovered somewhere wiped clean of fingerprints, it's just part of the woodwork so to speak. Chances are she'd never use that bottom platter. Even with their first-rate cabinets, it's hard to bend all the way down to reach that one.

And with all the other platters easier to reach, why even bother?"

"I'm not saying it's not clever, just that it might not help us all that much."

"But if it points to Freddie in *any* way, maybe it'll convince you to focus on him instead of Hal. And are you telling me that if Essie Sue swears that platter is hers, and if she might even have more like it, you wouldn't be swayed? And maybe it has some identifying marks on it that she can point out to us."

"Let me think about the best way to secure it," he says, giving me the familiar look he uses when he knows I'm onto something but, for his own reasons, he isn't ready to admit it. It's half grin and half grimace.

"Think away," I say, "I'm out of commission for this evening anyway — I have to go take that sleep apnea test I mentioned to you the other day."

"You haven't fallen asleep at the wheel, have you?"

"No, my doctor is trying to forestall that. My symptoms right now are that I have interrupted breathing when I sleep, and sometimes I awake with the feeling that I'm not getting enough air in my lungs. If they discover I do have sleep apnea, I'll be trained to sleep with a breathing mask at night. A drag, but it's better than having a sudden stroke in the wee hours of the morning. Of course, I'm hoping I pass the test and don't have it."

"Is the test given at the hospital?"

"No, it's at an independent lab the doctors here use. A little converted house on Byron Avenue. I have to report at nine tonight, and I'm finished by six in the morning. *Then* I'll noodge you about the platter at Freddie's."

"I don't want the man alerted to anything right now, Ruby — just hold on, okay?"

"I'm perfectly happy to hold on, Paul," I say. "You're running the show here."

"Yeah, that's what Eve said to Adam when she handed him the apple."

23

It's nice outside and I've decided to leave my car at home and walk, carrying my overnight bag with me. Although I'm not looking forward to this testing, I can count at least two positives. For one, I'm missing the evening's reunion event in Austin — the traveling exhibit of Jewish ceremonial art that I've seen on several occasions already and found to be boring even the first time. The only thing that filigree and sterling silver does for me is to initiate depressing thoughts about silver polish and elbow grease. I advised Essie Sue against considering this as an evening's entertainment, but we all know where she files my advisories.

The other good thing about tonight is that the testing facility is so close to my house — just a few blocks away. Before I checked out the address, I'd never noticed the place. It's located in a neighborhood adjacent to mine, and it's zoned for residence and business. You'd miss the house entirely if you weren't looking for it, and I almost bypass it this time, too, before seeing a couple of cars parked in front —

one empty and the other with a person who seems to be waiting for someone inside. The small sign above the door says ETERNAL SLEEP SYSTEMS INC. — sounds like a funeral home or a cryogenics outfit. Hoping I'm not ready for eternal sleep just yet, I step onto the small wooden porch and ring the bell. While I'm waiting I almost step through one of the floorboards, which should give me a clue, but doesn't.

A huge guy who looks like a wrestler opens the door. He's wearing a bright blue shirt that I think is supposed to be a uniform, except that it's about two sizes too small for him. It turns out that he is a wrestler, or used to be, because I ask him. He explains that he's an ex-wrestler. It's unclear how he's made the transition from the ring to the sleep business. No one has prepared me for what to expect, and I get a sinking feeling when I realize I've come to spend the night with this person, or at least in his vicinity.

What was formerly the house's living room is now a computer facility — two big computer screens with CPUs and printers are set up on long tables, being monitored by someone who's obviously yet another wrestler.

"I'm Darryl," the first one tells me, "and

I'll be your attendant. I'm the client technician." He points to the other guy. "This is Long John. He'll be monitoring your sleep patterns on the screen all night. We have your paperwork already — the doctor's office sent it over."

To say I'm anxious would be less than an understatement.

"So it's just you two?" I say, thinking of where I'm going to have to put on my pajamas, not to mention what else might be on the agenda. There's something about being alone at nine o'clock at night with two enormous strangers that's somewhat off-putting, even if my doctor did send me here.

"Yep, just us. There's one more person in the second sleeping room through your other door and out the hall — he started his test at eight."

I feel so much better now knowing there are three men here with me instead of two.

"I just assumed there'd be female attendants," I say.

"There used to be one, but there was a budget cut and I had seniority," Darryl says. "Things are looking up, though. We usually only have one client at a time in here, but this week business has picked up."

He leads me into what seems to be the second bedroom to get ready.

"Don't worry," he says, noticing I'm edgy, "you'll sleep like a baby. We have the room fixed up just like your bedroom at home would be."

Only if my bedroom were the shantytown version of Motel 6. Make that Motel 2.

The room is small, dim, crowded, and freezing. A queen-sized bed takes up most of the room — it's covered with your standard-issue motel bedspread, a dark print constructed not to show stains, and believe me, I'm not anxious to find any. There's no room to sit on the bed, however, because various instruments have been meticulously laid out on it — hoses, wires, electrodes, and two gas mask–type appliances. I stare but don't touch.

"Take off your clothes," he says, "and put on your pajamas. I'll be back."

"It's cold in here," I say.

"We have a new space heater. It's in that box," he says, pointing to an unopened box in the corner on his way out the door.

So am I supposed to set up the heating system on my own? He didn't say. I look around some more and see a thirteen-inch black-and-white television set that looks like it was made around the time of the "Milton Berle Show." It has an antenna pointing sideways, and I discover it will only broadcast a ragged version of the religious channel. It's plugged into a broken wall socket — the sole outlet in the room. I imagine I'm expected to connect the heater to the bottom plug of this socket if I don't want to freeze, so I have a choice between the cold and any heat produced by a possible electrical short.

Not knowing what to expect, I fortunately threw in a pair of long-sleeved flannel pajamas when I packed. I keep my socks on when I change, and I'm still colder than ever. I'm tempted to open the new space heater, but prudence tells me to let Darryl take charge of that. If anything goes wrong, it'll be the lab's responsibility, not mine. I try to keep the word *firetrap* out of my brain, but like the proverbial elephant in the room, it's there anyway.

Darryl knocks discreetly on the door and opens it indiscreetly at the same time.

"Ready to get started?" he says.

"Could you unpack the space heater? And is there another plug hidden away somewhere that you could use?"

He's annoyed now, but trying not to show it. He opens the box, unplugs the television set, and hooks up the heater to the top part of the broken socket.

"Okay, here's what we do now," he says, pointing to a small space near the foot of the bed. "You sit here, and I'll attach these electrodes to your body. I have to use sticky cream and it might be cold."

I sit and try to be blasé about a male stranger reaching into the neck of my pajama top and attaching two electrodes connected to wires to the top of my chest. He follows through two by two on my legs, arms, and various other places. The grease *is* cold, and the space heater doesn't seem to be helping. When I'm thoroughly connected with wires trailing all over my body, he helps me up and leads me to the head of the bed where I'm supposed to get in.

"Do you have to go to the bathroom?" he asks.

"Now?"

"I forgot to mention it before," he says. "Luckily, I haven't attached the other end of your electrodes to our computer outlets. So do you?"

"Yeah, as a matter of fact, I do. Where is it?"

"You have to go down the hallway and step outside for a few feet."

"You mean around the corner like at a

gas station?" I say.

"More or less," he says, assuring me that unlike a gas station bathroom, this one is completely private.

"Private for whom?" I ask. "How about the man being tested in the other room? Does he use that bathroom, too?"

"Sure. But he went already. I doubt he'll have to go again — his wires got all snarled up when he tried to close the door behind him. He's not in such a good mood for his test, and he didn't listen to me. He's not with the program. I told him he should leave it open — I was watching for him."

"And who would be watching for me?"

"I'll turn my head if you go. It's still better to leave that bathroom door open so your wires can trail behind you."

I ponder for a minute the specter of me in my *Monster from the Blue Lagoon* getup, and decide I really don't have to go after all. No wonder the other guy was in a bad mood.

"Hook me up," I say. "I don't have to use the bathroom."

"A lot of people decide not to," he says.

He launches me onto the bed and fastens each wire to the wall behind the headboard, where I assume it reaches the computer outlet.

"See?" he says. "We have a comforter on the bed so you won't be cold when you sleep."

"Sleep? I forgot I'm supposed to sleep."

"That's the purpose of this. After we attach all the mask equipment."

Now I can see why they hire wrestlers. He goes into the hall and wheels in a heavy cart filled with headgear, something that looks like a vacuum cleaner cord, and gas masks.

"For the first part of the test," he says, "we stick these probes up your nose to record your breathing rate. Later we try on the various sleep masks to see what works. They all require these straps, which attach to your head. Be careful not to let the straps get mixed up with the electrode wires on your cheekbones and forehead."

As if I have any control whatsoever.

"I'm turning out the light," he says.

"Do you have to?"

"Yes, you'll never get to sleep if I don't. Just let yourself drift off naturally, and we'll wake you later."

"You're kidding, yes?"

"Just relax," Darryl says. "Otherwise the test won't work and you'll have to come back and take it again. If you don't go into a deep sleep, the graphs we print out don't give us the right data."

"I'll never be able to sleep," I say.

"Sure you will. Would you like the TV on to calm you?"

"You mean I have my choice of the TV or the heater?"

"Oh, yeah, I forgot about the problem. Which one?"

"The heater. I can do without the sermon channel."

The key piece of information I've gleaned from all this is that if I don't sleep I'll have to do this all over again. I'm sure he said that on purpose.

"Just yell if you want me," he says. "We have the room all miked up and we can hear you. You'd be surprised at the things people say in their sleep."

Another terrific incentive to doze off. And I remember something else.

"I can't sleep on my back."

"You don't have to — roll over on your side if you need to. But with all those wires, I'll have to start all over if you detach any of them."

"I'll sleep on my back."

"Cool. Have a great night, miss."

24

"Darryl?" I don't think he can hear me in the other room, even if I am wired for sound. "Darryl?"

The door opens and Darryl turns on the lights.

"What time is it?" I ask.

"Eleven o'clock. An hour and a half after we started. You're supposed to let us worry about the time. We're getting no readings indicating you're asleep."

"Everything's getting numb."

"You can wiggle your arms and legs — everybody does it."

"Except if the wires detach, right?"

"Yeah, except for that."

"And this air forced up my nose is irritating my nostrils."

"Anything else, miss? And remember, you can quit if you want to."

He leaves before I can answer — he's good at this.

Unconsciousness is out of the question. Even if the wires weren't attached, I'd be awakened by the rock music station Darryl and Long John are tuned into on the other side of the paper-thin wall. I'm not asking them to turn it down because it reminds me that I'm still on this planet and not in the arms of aliens.

The trouble is, Darryl's used just the right psychology on me. The very first time he told me I could go home because some people can't take it, I was determined to stay. He gets the same pay whether I go home or not, with a lot less work, so why shouldn't he want me to drop out? I'm staying.

The next thing I know, it's two in the morning, and Darryl comes in to tell me I'm ready for the next part of the test.

"See," he says, "you slept."

"No, I didn't. I've been staring at the ceiling the entire night."

"Nope, we have it down on tape. You slept."

He takes the two probes out of my nose and replaces them with one of the gas masks I saw laid out on the bedspread earlier. He must have taken them off the bed before I climbed in.

He fits some loose Velcro straps around my head and attaches the mask to them. Then he connects the vacuum cleaner cord to the mask and plugs the other end into a piece of equipment beside the bed.

"Breathe naturally," he orders.

"I can't." I jerk the mask off so I can tell him that if I breathe through my nose and then try to open my mouth, the air rushes in and chokes me.

"You'll get used to that part," he says. "Just breathe through your nose and not your mouth."

He leaves me to my fate, or I should say *his*, after reminding me that I can get up and go home at any time.

Once I get used to clamping my mouth shut, I can sense the rhythm of the air coming through my nostrils — it feels a lot better than those nose probe things, and I relax.

I hear the hum of the machines as I half wake from what must have been a great dream. I remember walking on the RiverWalk in San Antonio with Ed Levinger — not just walking, but gliding along. We were holding hands and taking long leaps in the air — then soft-landing — sometimes on the water without getting wet, and at other times along the banks. I was very happy. We drifted in and out of the shops along the way, and in one, we bought crystal spheres like disco ceiling balls — put together with multicolored glass, and perfect for juggling.

I drop one of my balls and it crashes with the tiniest tinkle — like two glasses clinking together. The crash makes me open my eyes even though I don't want to. The room is black as ever, and the air seems heavy and hard to breathe. Up until now the fresh air rushing into my sleep mask has been moist and soothing, and in my half-sleep I expect the flow to continue in that same, rhythmic pattern. But it doesn't.

The thick, corrugated hose connected to the top of my sleep mask is pulled out of its socket with a whooshing sound, leaving the mask itself still strapped to my head, but useless. My lungs haven't caught up with what's happening, and I try to pull air through my nose as I was instructed. The socket in the mask is stopped up somehow, because I'm drawing in and nothing is coming through.

My mouth takes over — no mask blocking that, and I'm able to take a big gulp of air before a hand is clamped over my jaws, pushing them together. If this is a nightmare, it's an instant one, because the whole thing lasts only the few seconds it takes to draw in a breath three or four times. I try to push the hands away from my face and can't. It feels like forever, and

I'm caught in slow motion as the blackness in here gets blacker, if that's possible.

As quickly as it came, the pressure disappears. I must have passed out for a moment, though I'm not sure. I'm too limp to call out or to pull my mask off, so I just breathe in and out of my mouth until the dots inside my eyelids stop whirling. I keep thinking my pajama top needs wringing out — it's clammy next to my skin. Or maybe my skin is clammy, instead.

I'm finally getting it together enough to wonder why this lack of privacy I've been so worried about all night isn't working in my favor. I thought the guys in the front could hear my every word — Darryl said I was *miked*, didn't he? Of course, I haven't said a word, either, and everything I remember happening except that one small tinkling sound has taken place in absolute silence.

It takes every ounce of energy I have to pull off the mask so I can call for help, but the bright overhead light bursts on before I say a word. I'm so blinded I can't even see Darryl clearly. Long John's with him.

"What happened?" Darryl says. "The screen stopped recording your breathing. You're not supposed to be having apneas during this part of the test — the mask takes care of that."

I'm discovering I can't speak yet, but I can see that while Darryl's talking, he's looking around at the train wreck that's just visited me.

"What did you do to yourself?" he says. "Half this stuff's disconnected. Hey, Long John — help me get her hooked up again — she's made a mess of this equipment — the boss'll kill us."

My voice comes back in a hurry when I realize that sleep mask is heading toward me.

"Hold on," I say — a lot less forcefully than I mean to, but I'm still limp.

I sit up in the bed and fold my arms in front of me, holding off some imaginary frontal attack from Darryl and Long John.

"You don't get it," I say. "Someone cut off my air a minute ago."

"That's what we told you," Long John says. "Your breathing stopped recording on the screen."

"I'm telling you there was a person in here. I felt a hand on my mouth, and I couldn't breathe through the mask."

The two of them exchange a glance.

"This came up in our training," Long John says.

Happy as I am that they were trained, I

flinch as I see what's taking place here, and try to head them off.

"No way did I make this up," I say. "Something awful just happened."

"You had a nightmare," Darryl says. "We heard about this. They told us one guy didn't like being tied down and when he finally went to sleep, he dreamed he was being held to the ground. He flipped and went berserk."

"Yeah," Long John says, "why do you think we had to be strong to get this job? It's because we deal with big men sometimes, and you never know what they'll do in their sleep."

That answers the wrestler question, not that I'm interested right now. "Well, I'm not a man, and I'm not big. And I was having a peaceful dream."

"Just let us do our job, miss, and see what damage has been done." Darryl's heading toward the wall connections.

My senses are coming back now, and I realize that this could be a crime scene. I have to make sure these two don't start putting things back together.

"Okay," I say, "don't get excited." Great — I'm telling *them* not to get excited. But they're bigger than I am, and once they start cleaning up the room, I'm sunk.

"Wait," I say. "I'm the client, or patient, or whatever, and I'm upset. You have to calm me down — your bosses trained you for that, didn't they? That's a bit more important than getting the room in order."

"She's right," Long John says. He whispers something to Darryl, and I'm sure he's thinking my response will be part of any damage report.

"Okay," Darryl says. "Do you want some water? You're not supposed to have anything to eat or drink during the test, but . . ."

"Don't worry about that," I say, "the test is over. I'm going to be one of those people who leaves."

"It's five in the morning," Darryl says. "We got enough data on you already — you won't have to come back."

"Why doesn't Darryl go get me some water?" I say to Long John. I'd rather deal with just one of these guys when I get my cell phone out of my overnight bag.

I ask Long John to hand my bag to me, and as I thought, he's alarmed when he sees me retrieving my cell.

"It's okay," I say again. "I'm allowed one phone call."

While he mulls that idiocy over, I'm already on the phone to Paul — thanks to my speed dial.

"Paul, it's Ruby. Wake up enough to do what I say, okay?" I wait a second. "Are you conscious?"

He sounds awake enough to listen.

"I'm at the sleep center on Byron Avenue. I'm all right, but something's happened here, and I want you to talk to the technician with me — his name is Long John. Yeah, you heard it right. Tell him who you are and that he's not supposed to touch one thing until you get here. This is important."

I give Long John the phone and he listens.

"Yes, sir," he says, and then slumps as he says it again.

"Why did you have to do that?" he says, handing me back the phone. "Our boss is going to hate this. We might lose our jobs."

"You didn't do anything wrong," I say. "I'll make sure your boss knows you did good work. You might even get points for working with the police so well. And you didn't call them, I did."

This seems to placate him, but not for long.

"Where's Darryl?" he says. "The watercooler's in our office, and I know we had a supply of cups — I just put some out there."

193

That's all I need — for one of the witnesses to run off before Paul gets here — even if he didn't witness much. Maybe he's even tied into all this.

I get up and try to move toward the door, forgetting that in my wired state I look like something that's come out of a pasta maker. My breathing cord may have been disconnected, but the rest of me is joined to half the equipment on the wall.

I point at the door to the watercooler, and Long John gets my message. He goes to look for Darryl, and when he doesn't come back in a couple of minutes, I kick myself for possibly losing both of them.

Darryl finally comes in the door, without my water. Long John's following, trying to catch up with him.

"Where'd you go, Darryl?" he says. "With all this commotion, I need you here, man."

"You know that guy taking the test in the other room?" Darryl says. "Remember I said he was sleeping so much better than this lady here?"

"Yeah, what about him?"

"He split."

25

Until Paul walks into the room, I've forgotten how spectral and hydra-like I actually look. I try to duck under the covers, but the horrified expression on his face tells me it's too late. Just a few days ago I was speculating about where our occasional teasing might lead, but I guess I can forget about that. There's a reason witches don't flirt.

He has to sit down, and he lands on the side of my bed.

"Are you okay, Ruby? You look like —"

"Yeah, I know — like something the cat dragged in, an alien from the blue lagoon — any other cliché you ever heard," I say, trying to pull the sting before his demeanor changes from shock to amusement.

To my amazement, my eyes well up and I blurt out exactly what I'm most trying to avoid. "Don't you dare make fun of me, Paul."

"Ruby, I don't even know why the hell I'm here at five in the morning, but trust me, it's not funny."

Ignoring me for the moment, which is

probably a good decision, he turns to Darryl.

"Since Ms. Rothman's obviously upset," he says, "can you fill me in on this place and what happened here?"

"Nothing happened, mister, or at least, not from our end. We didn't do anything. This is Eternal Sleep Systems, Inc. — we have branches all over Texas, most of them bigger than this one."

Long John pulls a brochure from a bracket on the wall and hands it to Paul, who stuffs it in his coat pocket.

"World-class, huh?" Paul looks around, but doesn't go there.

"They tell us Eternal's lucky to have one at all," Long John says. "And we'd like to keep our jobs here. Do you think you'll be around long?"

"I just got here," Paul reminds him. "The sooner you answer my questions, the sooner you can get back to work. What happened? Was Ms. Rothman assaulted?"

"No, sir. People have some really weird dreams when they're taking the sleep test. She thought someone came in and blocked her air mask."

Self-preservation takes over and I recover — I'm certainly not letting these two tell Paul what happened to *me* when they were all the way on the other side of the wall.

"Okay, I'm back," I say, sitting up in bed trailing all my glory. He's seen the worst, so what difference does it make? I tell him every detail of what happened, ending with the part about the guy in the next room going missing.

"Somebody wanted to frighten me," I say.

Paul hasn't moved from his perch on the bed beside me, and even though we're only inches away each other, he sits his ground. I guess when you're a police officer, you develop a tolerance for apparitions.

"Or the person wanted to get rid of you," he says.

"I was asleep and totally powerless under that mask," I say, "and he wasn't interrupted, either. He could have taken a few more minutes to suffocate me, but he didn't."

"You don't think this really happened?" Long John says.

"I know Ms. Rothman well, and she's trustworthy," Paul says. "For the purposes of this morning's investigation, I'm going on the premise that she didn't have a bad dream. If she did, she'll remember that soon enough, but I want you to respond carefully to my questions. Just tell me what happened as you saw it."

Hmmm — Paul certainly isn't committing himself. I'm wondering if he *does* think I might have been dreaming, and just wants to be thorough.

"I need to get disconnected," I say, realizing that the more unreal I appear, the harder it's going to be to believe my story. "Let me get my clothes on before we go any further."

"I don't want anything disturbed in here," Paul says. "How about taking that zipper case into a bathroom?"

Darryl disconnects me completely this time, and I take my overnight case with me to the *convenient* outside bathroom. The air is freezing in here, and the cold concrete-block walls don't help. Trying to get dressed without touching anything is lots of fun, but I feel better when I think about how much worse it would have been to use this bathroom earlier with all my wires trailing.

When I go back to the testing room, Paul hands me a Styrofoam cup of coffee he's scrounged from the guys. At least with my jeans and sweater on and my hair combed, I feel like a human being.

"Okay, Ruby," he says, "I've gotten their

stories. I need more from you. I know you said it was dark, but did you sense anything familiar about this person — smell, feel, some other recognition? Maybe if you close your eyes and sit on the bed again, you can re-create it."

"No," I say, sitting down, "he was a stranger. And a man — I could feel the strength and just the grip in general. It wasn't a woman."

"Ruby's room has the two doors," Paul says. "He probably went out this side door, and he had to come in that same way — there's no window and he wouldn't have used the door leading to the computer room hallway."

"Hey, Lieutenant, if she wasn't dreaming, it could have been the guy in the next room — the other sleep client," Darryl says. "Then he made a run for it. But I know we would have heard something," he adds, rubbing the side of his head as if to get something going in there. "I still think she was having a nightmare."

I'm grateful that Darryl is at least willing to flirt with the possibility that this was real.

"He's wrong about it being the other client," Long John says. "I'm the main computer person in the front room. If that man had taken off his wires, my screen would have shown it in the same way I knew Ms. Rothman wasn't recording any breaths. We would have known."

Smart guy. I hadn't figured that out yet myself, although I can't say I'm exactly in full mental jacket yet. Paul, on the other hand, is way ahead of him.

"Yep," he says, "the timing's off. The guy in the other room left when you two were already on your way to Ruby's room, answering her call. But his room does have a window, and it's possible he saw the attacker come through his room, or even let him in. Why else would he take off like that?"

"How about your recording system?" I say. "You told me my room was wired for the tiniest sound."

"The lieutenant asked us for that stuff while you were out getting dressed," Darryl says. "We'll give him a copy of everything."

"Why don't we hear it now?" I say, looking at Paul. "I think I have a right to know if I was hallucinating."

"Oh," Paul says with that half-amused glance he throws at me all too often in these situations, "you mean you're now accepting the possibility that you were dreaming?"

"I'm accepting nothing. But we're here,

the equipment's here, and these techni-cians can have it on in a minute. Why should we wait?"

"Let's go for it," he says. "Looks as if I'm up for the day, anyway."

"*Oy*," I say to him while Darryl and Long John head for their machines, "this is the same day we're supposed to end up at the reunion banquet together. We'll be half dead by the time night comes and the dinner starts."

"Don't think about it," he says. "Just be thankful you're in good enough shape to go at all — it could have turned out worse."

Thinking of the alternatives, I have to agree with him.

"How am I going to hide all this from Ed tonight?" I say before I think about it.

"Ed's coming now? Does he know you that well to be able to tell when you're keeping something from him?"

"You mean the way you always have?" I say.

"I'm trained to do it," he says.

"So is he," I say. "He's a reporter."

My answers are quick enough, except that I'm getting an odd feeling that we're no longer talking about respective profes-sional skills here, but about who's closer to me. Darned if I know.

26

All I can say is thank heavens Ed isn't here. Darryl and Long John are fast-forwarding over the tapes of my night from hell, stopping at pertinent points along the way. I feel as though three men are now in bed with me, and figuratively speaking, they are. Every snort, wheeze, jerk, tumble, and turn I took tonight are recorded in full volume, and it's not pretty. Apparently, I did a fair amount of cursing, too, when the wires caught behind my ears as I made a futile attempt to roll over before I learned better.

Who knows *what* the heavy breathing was all about — since the night's experience from beginning to end was a complete turnoff, I was probably captured experimenting with mouth-breathing compared to the nose-breathing I was told to stick to. At any rate, I sound like the perfect bedmate, and from the look on Paul's face, I'll never live this down.

"Okay, so this was a big mistake," I say. "What's it going to cost me to keep this out of the station house break room? If those guys hear one iota of this waking nightmare, I'm coming after you."

"Aha — so now it's a waking nightmare," Paul says. "Can you clarify that?"

I can tell that Long John and Darryl, who're used to literally listening to this stuff in their sleep, are unfazed. "Okay," Darryl says, "this is the last part — before we came into your room to see what was going on."

The segment is preceded by a stint of regular breathing that confirms Long John's insistence that I did indeed fall asleep at some point. But listening to everything following that quiet time sends shivers all over me. First, there's the rustle of the covers as a strange pair of hands reaches out for me. The weird thing is that none of my listening companions can identify what's happening exactly, but I can, because I went through it only an hour or so ago.

I let out a groan in my sleep as I feel the pressure of a hand on the sleep mask, and then I awaken fully as I realize I can only gasp — that the air flowing from my mask into my nose has stopped completely. I remember now pulling against sturdy wrists, trying to force them back from my face. There's a whoosh as the hands disconnect the vacuum-like cord from the sleep mask, and then a plopping sound, which I think is something being stuffed into the hole in the mask where the cord was. Now, when I try to breathe through my nose, there's no air — only the small nostril-full caught in the mask itself.

The worst part can't be translated into sound at all — it's the strong hand pressing my jaws together so I can't breathe through my mouth, either. There's a weaker gasp on the tape at this point, when I try to suck air as it's being cut off completely. Other than that, I can hear no further sign of the fear I felt.

We listen to the part on the tape where Darryl and Long John come into my room to see what's the matter. The tape's still playing, but I interrupt.

"Could you tell from the sounds that I was in trouble?" I ask them.

"It happened fast," Darryl says, "and don't forget, we had the mike on all night — there were lots of sounds. What told us something wasn't right was your breathing line on the monitor."

Paul looks at me and I can tell he's doing an internal shudder, even though he's too well trained to let it show. It touches me.

"What's that?" Long John says.

"What's what?" Darryl looks at him.

"The tape. There's more going on."

"You mean after you came into my room?" I say.

"Must have recorded after we'd left the computer room and were heading down the hall to your room."

Paul's antenna is up all of a sudden — he points to the tape recorder and has Long John rewind to the part where my air appeared to be cut off. This is the point where Long John and Darryl must have been realizing I needed help There's some rattling and wheezing going on, and then the rustling of bedcovers. That noise had to have happened while I tried to push the attacker's hands from my face.

I wasn't able to speak, since I'd been asleep and also still had the mask on, so it's a surprise to all of us when the word *Damn!* comes up on the tape.

"That's a man's voice, not yours," Paul says. He has Long John play it over a few times, but it doesn't refresh my memory.

"I think I fainted at some point," I say, "and I don't remember hearing anything. Unless it was one of the guys coming into the room."

They both shake their heads *no*.

"It wasn't us," Darryl says, "I'm sure of it."

"Doesn't even sound like us." Long John plays ahead a bit, and we hear the door to the computer room hall open, Darryl coming in, and Long John following.

"Whoever it was had to have run out that side door," Paul says. "My guess is he went back into the other sleep-testing room and out the window of that room. If not that, he could have run out the front door while you two were in Ruby's room — you wouldn't have seen him."

"But we do have him on tape," I say, "and maybe that can be valuable to us. Aren't there sound wave comparison tests?"

"Yeah," Paul says, "but those are iffy with just the one word to go on. We could have better luck using that information to scare a suspect into thinking we had him on tape, if it ever comes to that."

We're all silent for a couple of minutes — each reaching for answers, I guess.

"Can I go home now?" I say.

"Wait a minute," Paul says. "I know you've had a hard night, but while the event's still fresh, I want to stay here for a little longer. Something's nagging at me."

We wait again while Paul drums his fingers on his knee. I've seen him do that a zillion times — better than scratching his head, I've always thought.

"Why would he say *Damn?* He said it before the guys started out from the computer room, so it wasn't that he heard them coming down the hall. At least I think that's the sequence — there's a gap on the tape between the *Damn* and the commotion when you two opened the door."

"So?" I say.

"Maybe you hurt him," Paul says.

"You think? I was pretty weak and sleepy."

"But you weren't sedated in any way, and you *were* fighting for breath. Whether you remember it or not, you could have done something that surprised him. Then he said *Damn.* Then he heard the guys coming down the hall and he ran out the other door."

Paul grabs my hands and takes a quick look at my fingernails.

"Do you have any rubber gloves?" he asks Darryl.

"A whole boxful."

"Come on, Ruby, let's go down to the station now. I want your fingernails examined."

"I thought I could go home and get some sleep, finally."

"Later."

While Darryl gets the box of gloves, Paul looks at the sheets and blankets.

"I'm sealing this room and the one next door," he says. "Maybe you dug your nails into his hands. We'll look for blood, prints, and whatever."

"You think this is all connected to the Max Cole killing, don't you?" I say as we get ready to leave. "Otherwise, you wouldn't be spending this much time on an assault that could be a dream, right?"

"Do you think it was a nightmare, Ruby?"

"Not a chance in hell."

27

Paul and I pull up to a ramshackle driveway a few blocks from Stone Avenue, quite a ways past Blue Feather Bridge. It would be quiet here even if it weren't Sunday morning — the street has a rural feel. These funky West Eternal neighborhoods can fool you — if you try to size up the occupants of the houses by the way they keep their lawns and porches, you'll be wrong at least half the time. This house has two raised vegetable beds in place of a front yard. They're weeded, watered, and neat, unlike the adjoining driveway, which is a receptacle for rusty wheelbarrows, oversized watering cans, bags of bonemeal and blood meal, and black trash bags full of dead shrub cuttings.

A man in sandals, shorts, and a surprisingly preppie blue-striped oxford button-down shirt answers the door when we knock. His legs and thighs are goose-bumped from the blast of cold air on the porch, but he seems not to notice. A kid on a tricycle circles the hardwood floors in the living room behind him, almost bumping into Tim Russert's looming face on "Meet the Press." I look at him and instantly decide he's not the man who attacked me. Paul, who has more professional obligations, can be counted on not to jump to my hasty conclusions. Still.

I asked Paul to interview this man soon — Carlton Fazio, whose name and address Long John furnished after only a faint whimper about confidentiality. Paul owes me, since I went through the long, dragged-out process at the station to disgorge the contents of my fingernails. It took some doing, though, to convince him I was no longer dying to go home and nap after my ordeal at the sleep center. Not that he was the least bit surprised — we're both wide-awake when there are gaping holes in our theories and a chance to fill them in.

"Can we come in, Mr. Fazio?" Paul says more than asks after he's identified himself.

As I introduce myself, I notice he's wearing a big silver ring on one hand and a wedding ring on the other. I decide to pounce before he gets his bearings or makes any judgments about me. I'm not sure if Paul'll approve, but it just seems to me that this is a good opening, while he's absorbing the fact that the police are here.

"Wow, what a beautiful ring. Did you have it commissioned by a silversmith?"

I take his hand and look at both sides of it as I admire the ring. Then I grab the other hand, asking if this is another one.

"Oh, I guess this one's just your wedding ring. But that's an amazing piece of work. Is it local?"

Paul's doing the equivalent of rolling his eyes while keeping a straight face — after all these years I know his gestures as well as Oy Vey's. He doesn't like my technique. I, on the other hand, feel as though I've won the marathon. I've examined both the guy's hands in the time it would take to say what a nice house you have, or child, or whatever. It's something I could never have gotten away with after the first two minutes here.

"Uh, my wife gave it to me for my birthday," he says. "What's all this about?" he says, looking at Paul.

Paul sits him down and goes into the whole megillah. I figure Carlton Fazio was either named by a first-generation American parent who wanted a classic Anglo moniker for the new American offspring, or was the product of a mixed marriage. He seems surprised when Paul tells him I was the one at the sleep center last night.

Now I can see that my ditzy opening doesn't jibe with my image as someone who was victimized only hours ago. Since both are true, though, I don't worry about it. I do make note of the fact that Carlton doesn't look tired — something I'd consider a common by-product of the sleep center.

He's telling Paul how well he slept with the mask, and I remember Darryl saying that unlike me, Fazio wasn't awake most of the night.

"Why did you leave the facility, Mr. Fazio?" Paul suddenly asks him.

"Well, I had to babysit my son while my wife went to the early church service this morning, and I just left while the attendants were handling what seemed to be an emergency."

Paul just looks at him. Those looks usually prompt a response, unless he's dealing with a sociopath, which this guy isn't.

"Don't you believe me?" The man tries to look outraged, but doesn't come close to bringing it off. Carlton Fazio is a nice guy. And P.S. — his hands don't have a scratch on them. Paul saw it, too.

"An attack was perpetrated on Ms. Rothman early this morning by a male suspect whose voice we have on the sleep center tape, and you were in the very next room. And you were the only other person scheduled in the building at that time."

"You mean you think it could be me? Come on."

Now I know it's not him — the real attacker would know he'd be a suspect in that situation. This guy's actually surprised he's being accused.

"You're all we've got, Mr. Fazio. Is this your story?"

Paul stands up and puts his hand in his jacket pocket where he's making something clink. If I were Carlton, I'd be figuring I was about to be handcuffed. He does.

"Okay, please sit back down. Bobby, go ride your trike in the dining room."

Paul sits. I never got up.

"Look, sir, I've got a family. The guy told me not to say anything. So I went straight home."

"Why don't you tell me the whole story as it happened?" Paul says.

"All of a sudden it's hitting me that you're not going to believe this," Carlton says. "I don't have any proof of it. Maybe that's what the guy wanted."

"You're not the police, Mr. Fazio. You don't have to worry about anyone's motivation — that's our job. You are expected to be truthful, though. Just tell me what happened."

"I was sound asleep with the mask on, and they were still taking my recordings, I guess. I'd been up earlier and Darryl had come in to adjust something, but I was back asleep. I'm a heavy sleeper."

That's putting it lightly, I'd say.

"I wake up because I hear a noise, and a man's climbing through the window. He must have crept in very quietly, because I didn't hear a thing until he was mostly through the window and bumped into something. He has a black Halloween mask on his face — just black with the eyes and nose cut out. I was groggy, but I could tell he jumped back when he saw me, like he didn't expect me to be there. He stood in the middle of the floor for a minute, trying to get his bearings.

"When I tried to reach for the buzzer to ring Darryl, or I suppose I could have just called out for him, too, but I was so groggy, the guy grabbed my hand and stopped me," Fazio says. "Then he put his hand on my neck like you'd wring a chicken and gestured with the other hand in his jacket pocket, like there was a gun in there. I figured he was robbing the computer equipment or something, and that he'd use the gun on Darryl and Long John, too.

"I should've called out, but I was frozen, and he offered me an out. He pointed to the window, and made me climb out of it. I grabbed my overnight bag and left. He leaned his head out the window and mouthed to me that *You talk, I shoot,* and he put his hand on the gun in his pocket. My car was in front and I drove off. I've got to tell you that I was glad to get away. I didn't even think of telling anybody. I was hoping I'd never see him again."

28

Paul and I are sitting in his car about to scarf down a McMuffin. It dawned on both of us after we left Carlton Fazio's house that we were starving, but this is ridiculous — with The Hot Bagel around, what we're doing is actually sacrilegious. But not irrational. My first thought was to make us breakfast at home, but I'm paranoid that Ed might come back up to Eternal early for tonight's banquet — he gave me no warning on Friday, either.

In my fragile and sleepless state I can't deal with him finding Paul and me cozying up to a cup of coffee around my kitchen table at nine in the morning. If Ed and I could have actually had the day together, that would have been something else, but there's too much on the agenda today to even think about that. Not that he ever gives me the choice — he either shows up early when he feels like it, or late because of work assignments. I'm hoping he can stay tonight, though — heaven knows we need the time together. I also can't afford to have Ed's famous nose for news sniffing out the works yet — it's too early in the investigation, and I don't need Paul to tell me that.

If I took Paul to The Hot Bagel for breakfast, we'd have to share our thoughts not only with Milt but with half of Eternal — at this hour, the unchurched half, I'd have to say. We also get a crowd at Sunday noon when all the worship services in town let out — bagels have no affiliation.

The coffee happens to be great here, and I'm so hungry, the McMuffin could be McCardboard and I wouldn't care. At any rate, I'm about to find out — Paul passes our paper trayful over to me and pulls over to the edge of the parking lot.

"So what now?" I say to Paul. "The Fazio lead's not going anywhere."

"I agree. Fazio saw a guy in a mask who didn't even say anything to him."

"We're not sure of that."

"Yes, we are. If the man had spoken inside the room, we'd have it on tape. He didn't, just like Fazio told us. I checked with Darryl."

"Let's brainstorm about what could have been going on," I say.

"You mean if it were your favorite suspect," Paul says. "Okay, speculate away. This is the time for it."

"Don't you have any ideas?" I say.

"I have plenty — some I'm ready to share, some I'm not. But you feel free — you're going to, anyway."

"I think Freddie started worrying in a big way when Kevin told him Friday night at his house that I'm helping the police with the Max Cole murder. That aspirin excuse, where he caught me in his study, would have worked beautifully standing alone. But not when combined with the fact that I'm helping with the Max Cole thing."

"And who did appoint you? Certainly not me."

"Be cute later, Paul. None of that matters, because Kevin said I was involved. I think Freddie saw an opportunity to scare me off, and since Kevin told him Max Cole might have been a criminal, strong-arm tactics might prove that point as well as convince me Max had dangerous friends."

"I don't think Freddie'd have the nerve."

"We have no idea what's at stake here for him — nerve could be the least of his worries. And breaking into a place where sleep tests are performed isn't exactly like cracking Fort Knox — I doubt he was afraid of armed guards."

"You did say he'd been there before."

"Yeah, he probably had his test in that room with the window, and remembered it'd be easy to get in. My guess is he expected me to be there just like he was. And I remember Darryl saying they rarely had two clients at the same time, so how hard could it be to find me? I think he did exactly what he came there to do — cut my air off enough to put the fear of the Almighty into me. The only unexpected complication was Fazio, and Freddie handled that pretty well, too."

"It's possible we can use Fazio to imply we have more than we do have in the way of identification," Paul says. "But we're so far from that step that it's not even worth talking about."

"We need some sort of plan to catch Freddie," I say.

"Brilliant, Ruby."

"You know what I mean. Just because I'm inarticulate this morning doesn't negate what I'm saying. With all these bits and pieces of evidence — the tray, the attack on me, and maybe my fingernails on his hands, I'm hoping we can think of a way to get him to reveal something more."

"Your fingernails," Paul says. "Maybe

the lab jumped to it, even if it is Sunday morning.

"Shit," he says while he's dialing, "I'm getting the phone all greasy."

I hold his breakfast while he calls. He's smiling when he hangs up.

"First real luck we've had. There were traces of blood and skin under your nails."

29

E-mail from: Nan
To: Ruby
Subject: *Re: I'm Fine*

I'm furious with you — you deliberately wrote me this in e-mail so you wouldn't have to hear me respond in the flesh, and aren't answering my calls on your home phone or cell. These are the times I hate caller ID.

Are you *sure* you're okay from that ordeal at the sleep place? At least write me back with more details — I hate it when you leave me dangling like this.

E-mail from: Ruby
To: Nan
Subject: *Take It Easy*

First, this wasn't my fault. You're acting as if this is one of those times when I took some huge risk and it didn't pan out. Remember, I was sleeping peacefully (well, not so peacefully) when all this happened to me. I didn't dare him to come after me, so be furious at him, not me.

I'll forgive you enough to tell you that I have a plan — actually, a couple of plans — as to how to get more information about Freddie. And I'm acting on both of them with the express permission of the police. Namely Paul.

First, in a few minutes I'm going over to Essie Sue's house. She continues to insist she perform her chairperson duties as if the world weren't falling down on her head. A couple of days ago, she asked me to help her fold a bunch of banquet programs, menus, and other printed matter she's foisting on the reunion guests tonight. At the time, I used the excuse that Josh was here, but now Paul and I have decided we need more information from her. She's kept tabs on the Fenstermeisters for years, and we think she can fill us in on more of Freddie's financial dealings.

I called her and found out that poor Hal was being pressed into service in my stead, and that now he can go upstairs and take another nap, which is what he's doing frequently now as his response to this whole situation. She has people she could call to help her, but she didn't want to have to bring up the whole murder thing with the other temple members. Of course, she continues to feel competitive with Freddie, who's gladly calling meetings without her.

I'll tell you the second plan when you write back and let me know you're not angry with me.

E-mail from: Nan
To: Ruby
Subject: *Spill It*

You're maddening, you know that? I'm just worried, as you well know, and no, I'm not upset with *you*, only with what happened.

But I am warning you to keep away from danger now that you've been targeted. Let the police do it.

Now, talk!

E-mail from: Ruby
To: Nan
Subject: *Second Plan*

My second plan, also blessed by the police, is a killer, you'll pardon the expression. Paul wants to see if there are any scratches on Freddie's hands without raising any alarm. *And,* you'll be happy to know, he doesn't want me anywhere near Freddie. He thinks I'd make him nervous in the extreme, even though Freddie has no reason to think I know he was the one who attacked me. Plus, he doesn't want Freddie to have an excuse to go after me again.

Paul eliminated himself as the person to see Freddie, since we don't want police presence around him — even an innocent handshake. Kevin would be awful, of course, I'd be worse, and Essie Sue a disaster. Paul was thinking of an undercover cop, when I came up with a better idea. Even the cop would have to make up a story, while my choice is a natural.

Freddie loved the idea of having our reunion at the same hotel as KillerCon in Austin. I told you he tried to invite some of the mystery authors to his suite for drinks — especially the more celebrated ones. No luck there — they had their hands full with their own stuff, although some of them weren't above being plied at the bar in the cocktail lounge.

My friend from high school is one of the convention speakers — Josie Joaquin — you know her books, right? I sent you her first one years ago. I'm positive Freddie knows her, too, and has seen she's a *macher* at the meetings. She finally got in touch with me — I've been leaving her messages. I asked her to help us, and she's arranging to run into him in the hotel lobby. She's going to tell him she's just come from a workshop, and she'll kid around enough that she'll be showing him how she was fingerprinted, using his hands to show him what could go wrong.

This woman is shrewder than I'll ever be, and I have no doubt she'll come through. He'll never think she's part of any plan, and all we want is a look at his palms — that's where my nails would have dug in. Even if he winces or suddenly doesn't like it, she'd surprise him enough to get a look, and that's all we want at this point.

I'll keep you posted.

30

I didn't think I'd live to see the sight that greets me as Essie Sue answers the doorbell, although I had a warning as I drove up the walk. Her always-meticulously manicured driveway was as ragged as her nails would be if she missed her weekly appointments.

"Come in, Ruby. You were a lifesaver to call this afternoon."

Uh-oh — already we're setting records here. I can't remember the last time she expressed gratitude for anything I did — and that's undoubtedly because there wasn't another time — this is it.

"I thought Hal could use a nap," I say, feeling an unfamiliar twinge of guilt at the meager excuse I've used. Not to worry, though — she isn't noticing. Her chic every-strand-in-place haircut is a thing of the past — I'm not even sure she's combed it today. And do I see roots showing? I look more closely and decide I'm wrong, but I'd swear they were on their way up. She's thrown on a blouse that doesn't go with her pants exactly — a no-no in Essie Sue World. All in all, I'm stunned.

She leads me into the study, where the *Architectural Digest* copies are strewn all over the table instead of being deposited in pristine layers. There's a musty odor in here, too. She clears the table for us by sweeping the magazines into the hammered-copper wastebasket.

"You're not throwing those away?" I ask — horrified but determined not to show it.

"No, it's just temporary," she says, apparently unfazed. "We need the room to fold the menus and program notes." As if that would have ever displaced her arrangements before.

"Hal's asleep," she says. "I don't want him to hear this," she adds, "but we're cash poor right now. I had to scrimp on some expenses in order to pay the lawyers. He's too depressed to deal with it."

"Why don't you let the other committee members take over the reunion activities?" I say. "You couldn't have a better excuse — everyone would understand."

I immediately backtrack — "Not that they'd do as good a job as you would, but at least you wouldn't be swamped at a time when you have so many other things on your mind."

"No, it's good for me. And if I withdrew, people would think Hal's guilty of something when he's not, Ruby. Besides, this reunion was all my idea, and I want to make sure it goes the way I planned."

That I understand — at least the Essie Sue I know hasn't disappeared altogether. She doesn't want to give up control just yet.

As if I needed any proof, she assigns our duties for the afternoon and gives me my folding orders. I'm relieved — it's disorienting enough in this house of unfamiliar dust bunnies and leftover coffee cups.

Sitting and folding is perfect for my plans. I hate to do this, but I need to get her started on Freddie, which shouldn't be a problem.

"Maybe Freddie and Francie can do more," I say. "He *is* your cochair."

"Not a chance," she says. "He's gloating enough already over our misfortune."

"He's got a lot of money," I say. "And Hal told me he'd done deals with him before. Maybe he could help you out financially and just call it a business arrangement."

"He's the last person we'd go to for help. I know too much about Mr. Fred Fenstermeister."

"What's he into, anyway?" I ask as casually as I can get away with. "Surely the hat business disintegrated with black-and-white movies."

"Oh, that — that's over and done with. Hal thinks his money's tainted."

"In what way?"

"He did deals for years with some people in Ohio and Illinois he was always vague about. When he wanted Hal to go in with him on some shopping center project, he wouldn't even tell him who the principals were. Hal laughed in his face. All I can tell you is that the Fenstermeisters would turn over in their graves if they knew how their money was being thrown around."

"So does he still have money, or do you think he's in debt to these shady businessmen?"

"We're not sure. He seems to have plenty — the way he and Francie live is lavish, but who knows if it's borrowed or his?"

"You know," I say, "Francie used to talk about the museum pieces they collected. Remember the two Fabergé eggs they had on display? And she hinted they had more. Maybe they sold their collection."

"Those eggs are fakes," Essie Sue says.

"How do you know?"

My fingers are hurting from folding this heavy card stock, but I'm afraid to quit while she's talking — I don't want to interrupt the flow.

"Hal said they were counterfeit, and believe it or not, Freddie admitted as much one time when he was trying to do a deal with Hal. I thought it was to get sympathy, but Hal felt Freddie really needed the money."

If he's been selling them off, I can see why he'd want people to think they were simply reproductions, despite Francie's bragging. But what I can't figure is how he got hold of them in the first place. Authentic Fabergé eggs are museum pieces.

"Let's assume," I say, "that they were real at one time. Could he have had the means to buy them? I never associated him with that kind of wealth, no matter how many deals he's claimed to have done."

"I don't know, Ruby. Why are you so focused on the eggs he had?"

Paul made me promise not to involve Essie Sue in any of the details concerning the computer chip we found, so I can't tell her more than she already knows. He's afraid of her big mouth, frankly, and I can't say I blame him. She could blab to Freddie if she knew what we were investigating.

"Just curious about the eggs," I say. "Fabergé always fascinated me, and they seem way too rich for Freddie's blood."

I manage to drop a bunch of the program notes on the floor as a diversion, and it works. Essie Sue's apparently not too out of it to lecture me.

"Slippery hands are a sign of sloth, Ruby," she tells me. "You'd be surprised how much a woman's visible traits reveal about her inner character."

You can say that again.

"By the way, Ruby."

Why is it that whenever this woman gives me a *by-the-way*, I get the shakes?

"FYI," she says, "I added a bonus to this afternoon's program for the reunion."

"I thought the crowd was going to the community center while we stayed here and did the paperwork for tonight's banquet."

I didn't shed any tears about missing today's event or, for that matter, the exhibit last night. The only reason Essie Sue planned these events was that she ran out of things for the out-of-town guests to do. The reunion's twice as long as it should have been — I'm thinking we shouldn't count on anyone desiring an encore for another fifty years at least.

"My latest plan will take place after you and I have finished with this folding project," Essie Sue says, "so we can both take part."

I'm afraid to ask, but curiosity gets the better of me, and I wait to hear.

"Some of the KillerCon people have graciously consented to have drinks with us in the cocktail lounge this afternoon and chat with us about mystery writing."

"What did you promise them?"

"Just hospitality, all the drinks they wanted, and a chance to promote their books."

Uh-oh — she hit the winning combination. What this has to do with our temple's saga, past and present, I don't know, but that's never stopped her.

"And I was hoping to rest before driving up to the banquet," I say.

"You don't have to come, Ruby — I can handle it."

You'd think with all Hal's troubles, Essie Sue would be looking for less to do, not more. As for me, I'm about to take her up on her pass to miss Cocktails with KillerCon in favor of a nap, when I suddenly realize this latest addition could screw up all my plans with my writer friend Josie Joaquin. I need to talk to Paul. Fast.

31

I'm feeling slightly schizoid as I walk into the hotel lobby carrying a change of clothes for tonight. I'll have to beg the use of someone's room to get dressed for the big *do*, but that's not why I'm nervous. As if today didn't bring enough of the unexpected, I've journeyed from Eternal just now with Ed, the latest surprise *du jour*. He drove up from San Antonio, and was waiting for me when I returned home from Essie Sue's this afternoon.

To put it bluntly, I didn't want to see Ed this early. I was supposed to save him a seat at the banquet in case he came up to Austin late — his usual MO. Any other time, I'd have been tickled to have the extra few hours with him and then drive up together. Today, though, his early arrival in Eternal — with no notice, of course — just means more awkward moments for me. Instead of real conversation, I have to make small talk with him in the car up to Austin — which I hate, so that he won't find out about my collaborating with the police. I've promised Paul not to reveal anything Ed could pick up on, but with his reporter's nose, this is no easy task. Not to mention my feeling like a hypocrite.

Fortunately, I had already called Paul from the car while I was driving home from Essie Sue's, so we'd had a chance to revise our plans before Ed arrived.

"I think it'll be okay, Ruby," Paul said to me, "it might actually be better this way. If your friend Josie is part of a group of writers talking to the temple people, it'll seem even more natural for her to interact with Freddie. Just make sure he's there — I'll get in touch with Josie and take care of the rest."

Now that we're in Austin, I'm wondering how I can find and talk to Freddie without Ed being around.

Ed squeezes my hand as we walk through the lobby. Maybe it's my imagination, but he always seems to be more demonstrative when Paul's in the picture, and the one thing he certainly does know is that Paul's working here today and I'm juggling my time between them.

"Your mind's in another place," he says. "What's up?"

This time I don't have to fake it. "We've got to pull the banquet off, Essie Sue's distracted and not herself, and this murder has cast a pall over the festivities," I say.

"Plus, this cocktail hour with the mystery writers has just been added to the schedule."

"Enough said," he tells me.

Great. He's extra nice just at the moment I'm feeling the most guilty. Why does it always happen that way?

"Thanks, hon," I say, shamefully deciding to capitalize on my advantage even more. "Can you circulate while I make sure our people know about this cocktail thing? I'll meet you after."

I'm off before he can respond.

Freddie's at the center of a knot of reunioners — monopolizing the conversation as usual. Since I don't dare to single him out, I take the opportunity to greet the group as a whole and ask if they know about the writers' session over drinks.

They do and are excited about it — probably because it's a lot more promising than the fare they've been given in the past few days, even if it has nothing to do with our weekend.

"Ten minutes," I say, deliberately flitting off without more conversation — ostensibly in search of others to tell. I know Freddie well enough to be sure he won't want to miss anything, so he'll be there. Josie should take care of the rest.

We've corralled four authors, three of whom are already sitting at separate tables in the bar. One is LaSalle Beaker, a Brit who hasn't written a book in years, but whose personal charisma still works its magic on two continents. He's already charming a table full of women over champagne cocktails.

The next is Stella Brenoff, a hard-working writer with two mystery series still going strong. I can tell just from looking that she'd rather be home curled up with her laptop than circulating, but she's smart enough to know she has to do both.

The third is Heath Abner, an author unfamiliar to me but obviously not to her fans, who're devouring her every word. They've ordered margaritas all round. Heath seems to have had a head start on them — her voice is up in the higher registers already.

But where's my friend Josie? I'm concerned that Freddie will come in and get pulled in by the wrong crowd if she's not here. Just to make sure, I sit at one of the empty round tables and try to save it for her, borrowing a bowl of popcorn from the bar to make it look inviting. I'll have to switch tables, though, when I see her coming.

I needn't have worried — she's on the case. Josie's a stunning, six-foot-tall brunette. I see her waiting at the door as Freddie's group appears — Paul has obviously clued her in. She strikes up a conversation with him in front of everyone and he seems flattered. She gives me a quick wink and slowly makes her way in my direction, giving me plenty of time to edge over to the perimeter of Stella Brenoff's gathering. She hasn't attracted as many people — probably because she doesn't seem to be having a very good time. I maneuver my seat to a spot where I mostly have my back to Freddie and Josie, but can still glimpse them in my peripheral vision. I relax and order a Michelob when I realize I'm the last person on Freddie's mind right now — he's engrossed in Josie's company.

The crowd joining Josie at the table includes a beloved editor who has her own fans. Lots of business is conducted at these conventions, Josie's told me, and some of the people here are practically standing in line to kiss the editor's ring — published and unpublished writers, agents, and younger editors learning the business first-hand. Josie told me if the popular editors carried home all the unsolicited manuscripts they're offered at these conventions, their planes would never get off the ground.

I can see, though, that this diversion is perfect for her purposes — Josie can spend some face-to-face time with Freddie and his group while the others are occupied. I can't tell what they're saying, but Josie seems to be regaling them with a story about fingerprinting. She's reached into her briefcase and pulled out a small jar of Vicks VapoRub. I'm fascinated, but trying to hide it by sipping my Michelob and smiling politely at the appropriate times during Stella Brenoff's banter at my table, if you can call it that. It's more like a monologue. Stella doesn't seem to be very good at witty repartee, although, not surprisingly, she's more successful in dealing with the substantive questions. Since I like her books, I'm sorry not to be more involved, but I've got other things on my mind.

Like watching in admiration as Josie takes not one but both of Freddie's hands in her own. He's keeping his right hand curled, but she teases and has his group laughing enough that he's letting her open one hand at a time and dip his forefinger into the Vicks. Then she reaches into her purse and pulls out a tissue, rolling the right fingertip back and forth on the tissue to illustrate whatever point she's making concerning the fingerprinting story. She does it again with another tissue she takes from her purse and uses on the left finger. I can see Freddie's been softened up by a few cocktails of his own — he has that slightly boozy look about him — enough to let down his guard. Not to mention that Josie is a master at this.

When she's finished, she wipes his fingers, balls up the tissues, and gives them to him — a stroke of genius, I'd say, just in case he was worried about having his prints taken, even in jest. I'm sure she got a good look at his hands. She even has the group clapping at the end. Since Josie so obviously knows what she's doing, I breathe easier and even manage to enjoy some of the conversation at my own table.

By the time our group has finished plying Stella with questions about her latest book and has managed to order two rounds of drinks, Josie's table has adjourned, except for a persistent agent who's holding the editor hostage while whipping out her Palm Pilot for an appointment. Since I know I can see Josie privately later, I want no part in following Freddie for now. The mission's either been accomplished or it hasn't, but we've given it a good try.

I'm sitting at the empty table deciding how long to wait before going back to the lobby when I see Ed walking toward me.

"I know I took a long time," I say, "but it couldn't be helped. I had to oversee this latest session."

"Where's Essie Sue?" he says. "I thought she was in charge of events."

I give him a blank look — things moved so fast I didn't even think about where she was. All I can do is be thankful — there's no way the author meetings would have gone this smoothly if Essie Sue had been here. I had originally planned to sit at whatever table Essie Sue didn't choose, and I knew I didn't have to worry that she'd join Freddie's group — they meticulously avoid each other. But I have to admit I felt blessed that she hadn't shown up at all.

"I can't imagine where she is," I tell Ed. Out of the corner of my eye I see Paul in the doorway. He heads toward our table. That's odd, too, because he pretty much stays out of my way when I'm with Ed —

even more so this afternoon, when he's trying to keep our plans secret.

Paul nods to Ed, but doesn't sit down.

"Hal Margolis was taken to the hospital," he says.

32

No one's in the hospital corridor when Ed and I arrive. I thought Sundays were busy visiting days, but Ed reminds me that it's five o'clock — visiting hours are over. Still, no nurses? No receptionists? The desk downstairs referred us to this floor after I used my clergy spouse routine to get us here, but I expected more activity despite the hour. The place is beginning to resemble that scene from *The Godfather* where Michael finds Marlon Brando all alone, when I see a figure emerge from the men's room. It's Kevin.

"I'm glad to see you," he says. "I went into Hal's room but no one was there — I guess they haven't transferred him from emergency yet."

"So you don't know anything?" I say.

"Yeah, I do," he says. "Good news there — it was only stress or something like that — no heart attack. He was having chest pains on his way to Austin."

"I left Essie Sue in Eternal," I say, "getting ready to drive up here herself. Surely she wouldn't bring Hal with her — he needed to rest."

"Well, she did," Kevin says. "She thought it would do him good to get out of the house, and she promised to let him stay in the hotel room while she ran around doing her thing. I'm not sure she was even supposed to bring him to Austin."

"Sounds real restful," Ed says. "I'm sure the poor guy was looking forward to pacing around in one room instead of his spacious house."

"Anyway, they were almost here when he got the chest pains — she drove him to the emergency room herself."

"I'd feel safer using an ambulance," I say, "but then again, when Essie Sue wants to get someplace fast, no one's going to stop her. I'm sure she made better time than the ambulance would have."

Kevin's doing a fair amount of pacing himself.

"Why are you so agitated?" I say. "You said he was okay."

"They'll be coming up here soon," he says. "I get nervous when I'm supposed to say the right thing to people — especially the Margolises. If he were worse, no one would be paying attention, or else they'd be appreciative I was here. What do I say when everything's all right?"

"First of all," Ed says, "I wouldn't say everything's exactly all right, Rabbi. The man's involved in a murder investigation, and now he's having chest pains from acute stress. And he's married to Essie Sue. I'd say that was plenty."

I have to agree. And sometimes the way Ed puts things makes me smile — he can be so sweet when he wants to. A lone nurse in blue slacks and a smock finally appears and comes toward us. At least, I think she's a nurse — she has that bearing. There was a time when the white uniform and matching stockings would settle that question, but those days are over. Now, only the ID pin tells for sure, assuming you're close enough to read it.

"Can I help you?" she says.

"We're waiting for Mr. Margolis to be transferred up here," I say. "Where is everyone?"

"We're short-staffed this weekend, but there should still be more than this. And there's a birthday party in the break room."

That explains it, but I can't help thinking they'll be glad they had that break when Essie Sue descends on them.

When Kevin walks over to the water fountain, Ed leans my way.

"What's the matter with the rabbi?" he says.

Kevin does look as though he's developed a tic.

"I'm pretty sure he's practicing his condolence call look," I say. "These occasions rattle him."

"After all this time?"

"He's made so many gaffes lately that he's paranoid," I say. "And you know he's scared of Essie Sue."

The elevator door opens and a wheelchair containing Hal appears, pushed by no less than three nurse's aides, followed by the recent subject of conversation. Now I know where all the staff went.

"Rabbi, Ruby, Mr. Levinger — in here." Essie Sue's sweeping gesture includes us and the assembled nursing personnel. She looks better than she did earlier this afternoon, though I can't imagine why. Maybe, though, she rises to the occasion when there are people to be bossed.

We dutifully troop after her while Hal is helped into bed.

"See, Kevin," I whisper, "she's not even paying attention to you. You're safe."

"No, she'll expect something significant from me, Ruby. You'll see."

As if on cue, Essie Sue turns to him.

"How about a prayer, Rabbi? A short one would be appropriate."

Kevin's panicking, but a voice from the bed saves him.

"Cut it out, Essie Sue," Hal says. "You heard the doctor. It's stress, not the Angel of Death."

"A few words wouldn't hurt," she says. "Go on, Rabbi."

"I didn't bring my book," he says. "I was in too much of a hurry." Kevin has a notebook with prayers for every occasion, since spontaneity is not his forte. "So let's just bow our heads in a moment of silent prayer for Hal's recovery."

Essie Sue glares at him, but I'd say he's pulled this off relatively well with the old reliable silent prayer.

Hal grunts his approval when we look up. "It *was* short, anyway," he says.

The nurse's aides seem uneasy about leaving, and I don't blame them. We all hover around the bed in an awkward silence.

Unfortunately, Kevin takes this opportunity to aim a so-called whisper at my ear. I know from previous experience that at these times privacy goes out the window — the man has never learned what a whisper really is.

"Ruby, Paul told me he wants to talk to me before the banquet. He said he has something he wants me to do. What's it all about?"

Essie Sue doesn't hear, but I'm sure Ed does, because he looks at me. At least I can answer Kevin honestly when I whisper that I have no idea what Paul meant. I'm thankful Kevin knows nothing about my writer friend Josie's performance this afternoon.

I'm trying to keep these plans from Essie Sue as well as from Ed for now. I'm thinking maybe I'll luck out when she's at the hospital tonight instead of attending the banquet.

That's not to be, however.

"I want to take a nap now," Hal says to Essie Sue. "You have to get ready for the big party."

"I have to stay here, of course," Essie Sue says, not too convincingly.

"The doctor says I need rest, and I won't get it if you're plumping up my pillows every two minutes. I'm ready for everyone to leave."

Two of the three nurse's aides take this opportunity to slip out of the room, and the third echoes Hal's words.

"Doctor's orders," she says. "We're

giving him a sedative for overnight. You can come back in the morning, Mrs. Margolis."

Essie Sue's caught between guilt if she doesn't stay and lack of control over the banquet if she doesn't go. I'm hoping the former wins out, but I'm pretty certain it won't.

"I *am* the Mistress of Ceremonies," she says with an expression that would be wistful if it were worn by anyone else. "So I suppose duty calls."

Hal's relief is audible — I doubt he's surprised, either.

The three of us leave the room while Essie Sue's saying her good-byes to Hal, and before we can go down the hall, Ed pulls Kevin aside. I was hoping he had forgotten Kevin's whispered words earlier, but of course he hasn't.

"What's Paul planning for tonight?" he says. Ed's no fool — he knows he has a better chance with Kevin than with me, but I make sure I'm still a part of the conversation.

"I just asked Ruby that," Kevin says.

"He just asked me that," I echo. "You heard my answer."

"Yeah, I heard you."

"So, Rabbi," he says, "what's happening

with this murder investigation?"

"That's what I'd like to know." Essie Sue's out of the room and into our faces without missing a beat, but this time, I'm really feeling bad for her.

"You see what this is doing to my Hal, Ruby," she says. "Something has to be done, and quickly. I don't think Hal can take too much more of this."

I'm having an out-of-body experience, or at least I wish I were. I'd give anything to be hovering anywhere else but here, veering between Essie Sue's forlorn looks on one side and Ed's accusing stares on the other. The trouble is, both of them have a point.

Where's Paul when I need him?

33

This is going to cost me big with Ed, but what else is new? I've called Josie and arranged to go to her hotel room while she's getting ready, so I can change clothes for the banquet. I couldn't think of another easy excuse to see her without Ed following me.

I'm carrying my garment bag and heading down her corridor on the twelfth floor when I hear footsteps behind me.

"Hey, Ruby — wait up."

It's Paul — not what I'd expected.

"*Oy,*" I say before I really think about it, "I just told Ed he couldn't come up here because it's a small room and we're dressing, and now you're here. How am I going to explain *that?*"

"With luck, you won't have to," he says. "Ed doesn't know about the rest of the investigation, so why would he have to know about this?"

"Because I've been silent about everything else, but I've already let him know I was coming up here. And that he couldn't come with me because it was women only."

"Don't be so paranoid, Ruby. You didn't

invite me here, Josie did. She and I have been in contact throughout this whole maneuver — once you introduced her to me, it was out of your hands."

"I'm feeling guilty as hell about Ed," I say.

"Sorry." He looks at me and decides he has to add something, I guess. "No — I'm not being flip — I really am sorry, Ruby. But Ed's a journalist — he's used to being out of the loop — his whole job is about getting inside. You know that. Why would he blame you?"

"Easy for you to say. Of course, he'll blame me. For finessing him all afternoon."

"What's going on out here?" Josie flings open the door to her room. "Hey, you two — I could write a lot more believable scene than this one. If you're determined to sleuth, don't you have sense enough to lower your voices? You sound like the Keystone Kops."

"Sorry," Paul says, "the conversation just got a little heated."

"Paul and I have a history," I say. Josie cocks her head and looks at me, as does Paul. I have no idea what I meant by that, but I think I'd rather drop it than explain it.

The queen-sized bed is obviously going to be our conference table — that's all the room holds besides the dresser and a chair. I hop on, kick my shoes off, and lean against the headboard with my legs stretched out. Josie does the same, leaving the foot of the bed for Paul.

"Ice bucket and water glasses are on the dresser," she says. "That's all I have except an Altoids."

Josie hasn't changed since high school — she's still unpretentious, practical, down-to-earth, and funny in an understated way.

"I thought I'd save time by informing both of you in one blow," she says. "Your friend Mr. Fenstermeister was happy to have me explain my writer's guide to the joys of fingerprinting."

"I saw the whole thing from my table," I say. "Looked as though you came through your demonstration without a hitch."

"And?" Paul says.

"He had scratches on both palms. I could see them plainly. Nothing special in terms of the hands being torn up or anything, but they did look pretty fresh to me. They were still red, not brown. He must have at least had to swab them with cotton or tissues to take care of any blood seepage."

I look at Paul. "See? I told you we'd get the goods on him."

He doesn't look as thrilled as I thought he would.

"Thanks, Josie," he says. "You were great. It's always messy, though, with this kind of evidence. I'll have to think about how I want to handle it."

"I'm way ahead of you," she says. "I wanted something a little more concrete, too. That's why I tried something on my own."

"What?" Paul says. I know he doesn't like surprises.

"I've got two color shots for you — one of each hand. I was afraid to take any more."

"You've got pictures?" I say. "Even when you had to use both hands to do that fingerprinting demo?"

Paul just looks at her — waiting for an explanation, which she seems pleased to give.

"My research involves personal contacts to a great extent," she says. "One of my new friends is a guy whose company has developed some really cool miniature digital cameras for use in investigative work. He let me bring one of them along to the convention. So instead of using it for my workshop as I had planned, I saved it for this favor you and Paul asked me to do. I'm wearing it right now."

Josie lifts an innocuous little silver star pin on her shirt lapel and turns it over. She shows us the smallest mechanism I've ever seen, attached to the back of the pin. It's even smaller than the phone cameras.

"A hole in the star pin is the lens," she says. "I trigger the mechanism from a wireless button on the inside of my waistband. All I have to do to take a picture is to push the button with my elbow. Since I've practiced this quite a bit since I received it, with very little effort I can aim the pin in the general direction of a close-up object, like Fred Fenstermeister's hands, trigger the release with my elbow at the waist, and get the photo. It's not complicated."

"Let's see the photos," Paul says.

"Can't you even thank her?" I say.

"Paul's like me, Ruby," Josie says. "He wants the bottom line, fast. The kudos can come later."

She pulls her laptop up onto the bed with us.

"I have them all ready for you," she says.

Sure enough, a close shot of each of Freddie's hands appears in living color on the screen. The scratch marks are shallow, but totally visible. With the evidence we've saved of the material under my fingernails, this should make a tidy package for Paul to give the Austin police.

"Now you can thank me," Josie says, distinctly flirting with Paul.

He reaches up and gives her a hug, but then gives me one, too.

"You found her for me," he says.

When Josie gives him the CD she's burned containing the images, we push him out of the room so we can get dressed for tonight.

"I'm psyched," I say to him privately before shutting the door. "Aren't you?"

"Yes and no, Ruby," he says. "I'd be a lot more excited if this were evidence of the Max Cole crime. We might be on our way to nailing him for the attack on you at the sleep center, but it'll mean nothing if he gets away with murder."

34

"He's awfully cute," Josie says as she slips on some leather pants for the banquet. With her long legs, they look great. Essie Sue will think they're over the top, of course, which makes them even more appealing to Josie and me. Since the KillerCon final event was last night, I've invited her to our dinner, and she's staying over this week for some postconvention workshops. Josie says the workshops are especially good this year, and are enticing a majority of the convention-goers. My hunch is Josie's glad she's here — she wants to be as close to the Max Cole action as possible.

"Yeah, Paul *is* adorable," I say, "but no more so than Ed."

"Methinks the lady doth protest and all that sort of thing," Josie says. "I saw the way he looked at you. Not to mention making a point of grabbing you so you wouldn't think you were being neglected when he hugged me."

"Don't be ridiculous, Josie. Paul was just being polite to hug me, too."

"Polite, no. Solicitous, maybe — I'll give

you that much, but it just proves my point. And by the way, when do I get to meet your Ed?"

"Oh, he'll be picking me up here or in the lobby — I'm supposed to call him when he can come up. Or when we'll come down."

"You look worried," Josie says. "Never fear — I won't spill anything. I know he's a journalist."

"The whole thing has me stressed out," I say. "Things are tense between us anyway, even without trying to keep this story from him."

"Is there dancing tonight?" Josie asks.

"Yes, sort of. You won't find many dancing fools in this group, I'm afraid — the average age of the band Essie Sue hired is pre-WWII."

"At least it'll be better than the buffet for thousands we had last night at KillerCon," Josie says.

"You're kidding, right? You had to stand in line instead of being served? With that crowd?"

"After the first twenty minutes, my friends and I left for the barbecue joint down the street."

"Well, you'll get good food tonight or the whole staff'll have to answer for it. Essie

Sue spent days up here having tasting sessions with the chef."

I'm just about dressed when my cell phone rings.

"Ruby? It's Paul. Is Ed there yet?"

"No. Why? He's going to call first to see where we'll meet — probably downstairs."

"Just wanted to make sure we could talk. And by the way, tell your friend Josie I said *hi*."

"Paul says to tell you *hi*," I say. Josie's eyebrows go on overtime.

"There's dancing tonight," I tell him. I start to say "Maybe you'll get lucky," but fortunately think better of it with Josie standing there.

"Listen," Paul says. "On the strength of what we've learned this afternoon, I'm resurrecting my idea about asking the rabbi to help us. I wonder what would happen if he let it slip to Fred or Mrs. Fenstermeister that he'd bitten down on that computer chip, and that you'd shared the information with the police? We've got to shake things loose here, and that might be a start."

"A start? You mean a bombshell. I don't know — do you want me to run it by Josie?"

"No. I realize she's hearing your end of

the conversation, but just tell her I said I wanted you to keep it confidential for now. I'm still considering it. It was just an idea, and I thought phoning your cell was better than trying to tell you downstairs with everyone around."

"Namely Ed."

"No, Josie, too. There's no reason she should be involved further, either. Just think about it. I'll get back to you in person or on the phone."

"Okay. Honestly, Paul, I have no opinion right now — one way or the other. Let's talk about it."

"I'd like that — it's just that the logistics are tricky tonight. We'll wait and see."

Paul's timing is perfect. Ed rings from the lobby just as I hang up from Paul, and we arrange to meet in the bar.

"You look great," he tells me when we kiss hello.

"So this is the famous Ed I've heard so much about," Josie says.

"Infamous, possibly," he says, shaking her hand and definitely not missing the leather pants.

"From what I hear, you're the celebrity," he says. "I'm sorry to say I haven't read your books yet, but I plan to rectify that — Ruby's raving about your latest."

"If you like it, how about passing it along to your book review editor at the paper?" Josie says, never missing an opportunity.

Ed laughs. "As one writer to another, I'm on the case," he says.

"Thanks," Josie says. "This guy's a keeper, Ruby."

"I'm glad he passed your bar," I say.

"Ha — I'm picking up the irony," Josie says. "I want you to know, though, that although one of my high standards might be that he like my books, I'm not blind, either, and he's definitely hot."

"That buys you the drink of your choice," Ed says.

We both want margaritas and he goes up to order them.

Before I can say anything to Josie, Kevin appears at my elbow. He must have been waiting for Ed to leave.

"Ruby, you've got to come talk to me for a minute. It's important. And it's private," he says, looking at Josie.

"I'm cool," she says. "Go. Don't trust me for too long with your boyfriend, though."

"Okay," I say. "Tell Ed the rabbi wanted me — I'll be back fast, I promise."

"Don't hurry," she says. "We'll be fine."

"That's what I'm afraid of," I say,

scooting before I have to explain anything to Ed.

Kevin takes my arm and practically shoves me into a corner of the lobby where Paul's waiting on a sofa that's partially hidden by a post.

"The rabbi insisted you be a part of this," Paul says. "We'll make it fast. Sorry to drag you away as soon as you came downstairs."

Kevin's not looking too good. Although he's dressed in his best black suit and wing tips, and has fortunately left off the black tie he wears for funerals, sweat's pouring from his temples.

"Lieutenant Lundy's been explaining to me what he meant when he asked me earlier to help out the police," Kevin says. "I don't think I like it."

"It might be the only way we can unnerve Fred Fenstermeister," Paul says. "He has no idea we've found the chip."

"But why do *I* have to do it?" Kevin says. "I told Ruby the other day that Freddie doesn't like me as it is — I don't need to aggravate him."

"This is a remark you'll be making innocently," Paul says. "How about saying it to his wife instead?"

"Better her than him, but she'll still tell

him right away," Kevin says. "And you know he'll pump me for more. It could be dangerous, too."

"You *would* have to be right on top of Kevin, Paul," I say. "He'd need to be assured that he was safe."

"That goes without saying," Paul says. "We'd set it up so that I'd be viewing the whole scene. There's no way I'd put him in danger."

"So what if you just made a couple of random remarks to Francie, Kevin," I say, "within earshot of a police person? This isn't a situation where you'd be soliciting a reply — all you have to do is to tell her about the chip casually. Then you could make an excuse and leave."

"What about Freddie?"

"We'll set it up so that you're just talking to the wife," Paul says. "You can let us worry about Fenstermeister."

"What if you sit at our table — Ed's and mine?" I say. "I'll make sure that you're surrounded by people — Paul can be there, too."

"I think that's a good idea, Ruby," Paul says, "arrange it so that we can all be at the table together."

"Essie Sue decided on first-come, first-served," I say, "no table reservations. I'll save some seats wherever Paul tells me to."

"How many people are at the tables?" Paul says.

"Six," I say. "There'll be five of us — me, Ed, you two, and Josie."

"I want another police person there," Paul says. "So count her in as the sixth. I'll call her right now, and she can show up as my date."

"Am I the only one without a date?" Kevin says.

"Josie can be your dinner partner," I say. "My writer friend you just pulled me away from."

"How do you know she'll do it?" Kevin says.

Paul and I look at each other.

"Oh, she'll do it," I say. "Josie'd kill to be in on this after helping us out this afternoon. I just hope she doesn't have to."

"Okay, I'll let that stuff slip to Francie. But you need to practice with me."

"Paul will do it," I say. "I've got to get back to Ed."

"Why?" Paul says. "Josie's good company."

"Touché" is all I can muster.

35

I'm sitting at one of these banquet tables wondering exactly how low I can sink. I had to turn down Essie Sue when she asked to sit with us, at a time when I know she needs the support. Our table was full, of course, and Paul had accounted for every seat. The lady cop from the Austin police who's his "date" dressed up for the occasion and looks every bit the great catch. Since Josie and Ed seem to have hit it off famously while I was meeting with Paul, the gods of retribution have, despite the seating plan, paired me with Kevin.

Even though I'm seated next to Ed and Kevin's next to Josie, Ed and Josie have arranged it so that the two of them are side by side as well. So it's Paul and Cutie Face Cop Betsy, then Kevin and Josie, then Ed and me. Ed's ignoring me, Josie's ignoring Kevin, and Paul's talking to Betsy instead of turning to me. That leaves Kevin trying to communicate with me across the table. He sure knows how to do *loud* — projecting his voice is one thing they taught in seminary that Kevin absorbed.

"Ruby, when is all this going to come off? Before or after dinner?" he pronounces.

I shrug my shoulders, trying not to encourage him. Fortunately, he's noisy enough to rouse Paul, who finally reacts by interrupting his conversation with Betsy and jamming his elbow into *my* side.

"Why me?" I say in a not-so-small whisper myself. "You're the one who's supposed to be in charge of him — don't ask me to keep him quiet."

Paul gives me an innocent smile while saying in my ear, "You're not jealous of my colleague here, are you?"

"You're enjoying this," I say.

"Enjoying what?" he says. "That your date is otherwise occupied? I'm sure Ed's just being as polite to Josie as I am to —"

"To your colleague?" I say.

"You told me yourself," Paul says, "that you felt guilty for keeping things from Ed."

"And whose fault is that? Didn't I have direct orders from the police not to talk to Ed about this?"

He finally wipes the smile off his face. "Okay, I'm being cocky. I'll move over in a minute and calm down the rabbi. But I do have something good to tell you — Betsy brought some interesting news with her from the station house.

"One of the hotel workers who was on duty the afternoon of the murder hadn't been questioned yet because he'd had permission to leave early for two days off. He'd left the hotel before he even found out about the killing, and when he returned to work last night, the manager sent him over to talk to us."

Kevin's looking restless again, and Paul leans over Betsy to tell him to hold on.

"I'll make this fast," Paul says, turning back to me and speaking close to my ear. "Anyway, this witness, Jim, saw a man entering the service elevator carrying a full silver platter. The man pushed the *close door* button and the elevator went up before Jim could get on. Jim said the man with the tray looked odd in that setting because he had on one of the giveaway T-shirts from the mystery convention. Jim was busy and didn't give it a second thought until we questioned him."

"Could he identify the man?" I say.

"Not so far. He thinks the guy was wearing a baseball cap pulled down."

"Not much to go on," I say.

"Yeah, but it's something. And at least it relates directly to the murder scene where we're missing a platter."

"Of course, the man Jim saw could have been Hal," I say. "Unfortunately, his height is the same as Freddie's."

"I'd better get over to the rabbi," Paul says.

"You can't just go sit by him," I say. "Ed's going to notice. And don't tell me Ed's too preoccupied with Josie — enough already. Why don't you let Policeperson Betsy spill some water on Kevin? He'll go to the men's room, and you can follow him."

"I guess it would work."

"Just don't spill too much — he'll freak out, and you need him to stay relatively calm."

Paul says something to Betsy, but before she can do anything, the waiters start serving the first course — soup. Now I'm worried Kevin'll get soup all over himself.

Paul one-ups me with a better idea — he excuses himself first and goes to the men's room — much less obvious than my plan. His colleague Betsy is carefully clever, too — I notice she backs up her chair before picking up her glass and spilling some water on Kevin — that way, his attention is focused away from the table and the soup.

"Hey — you messed up my new suit," he yells.

"I'm so sorry," Betsy says. "Why don't you use a bunch of paper towels on it?"

Kevin moves fast toward the men's room, and Betsy fusses around wiping his chair with her napkin. For the first time, I lean over and say something to Josie — I figure talking to Ed right now might be overdoing it.

"Did anything get on you?" I say.

"Not a drop," she says.

"How about your dinner companion. Did he stay dry?" I say. I can't resist the utz, and at this point, maybe it'll be a diversion.

"I thought the rabbi was my dinner companion," she says, and then belatedly gets the point. She doesn't embarrass easily, but this time I see her cheeks redden just a bit more than her blusher would produce.

"I'm cool with it," I say, laughing. Funny thing is, I discover I really am cool with it — I just wanted to zing her a little.

"What's going on with you two?" Ed finally says, looking from one of us to the other.

"Not a thing, darlin'. Having fun?" I say, and then answer myself — "Probably more than you expected, huh?"

36

Essie Sue's sitting behind us at a table with her cousins, although the word *sitting* is probably not accurate. She's jumping up every two minutes either to summon the maître d' or to give orders to a passing waiter. Knowing Essie Sue, she's feeling guilty about being here at all when Hal's in the hospital — so she's justifying her presence by making tonight work, not fun.

"You know, you can enjoy yourself, too, Essie Sue," I say to her when she comes by for the third time to see if our entrée has arrived. "Hal's getting good care — why don't you sit down and relax? You spent enough time selecting this food — you might as well have some."

"Where's the rabbi?" she says, ignoring me.

"He's in the men's room," I say, hoping that's a boundary she won't cross — not that I'm ever sure.

"He should be out circulating — I made him promise he'd circulate."

"I'll tell him," I say before she flits to the next table. I'm also realizing that for a change we can benefit from one of her mandates. Kevin's *circulating* can give him the perfect excuse to drop by the Fenstermeisters' table.

Paul and Kevin come back together, and Kevin's just about to sit down and eat when I tell him Essie Sue just stopped by.

"She wants you to — you know — circulate," I say with a quick look to Paul. He's with me on taking advantage of the opportunity.

"Yeah, go ahead, Rabbi," he says, "we won't let them take away your plate."

"But it'll be all cold, Ruby."

Paul and I are both afraid to say anything more, so we just look at him, and it finally dawns on him what we might mean.

"Okay, save everything," he says.

I can see him heading straight for the Fenstermeister table. Unfortunately, Freddie's doing some circulating himself and his seat is empty.

"That's good," Paul says quietly to me. "I prepped him on that — he'll take Freddie's seat and start talking to Francie. That could even be better — at least she'll give him a hearing."

"How much is he going to bring up?" I say, trying the mock chicken, which was two steps below the real food in price when Essie Sue made her arrangements. "Will he talk about the Fabergé eggs?"

"Just mentioning the chip should be enough to totally bum out Freddie when she tells him," Paul says.

"But what if Francie forgets to tell him?" I say, depositing the mock chicken bite in my napkin — it tastes just about the way I thought it would.

"Francie won't forget. I don't think this is something Fred could keep from her, Ruby — she's probably a part of anything he's up to. You should cool it," he says.

"Huh?"

"Cool it for a while. Talk to Ed."

I guess he's right — it's up to Kevin now, and I need to let Paul and Betsy do the monitoring. My safest bet will be to stay out of it and keep Ed occupied. Of course, Josie's done a pretty good job of that already, even though she's not in on our plans.

"I was wondering when you'd have anything to say my way," he says when I turn toward him. "You've been talking to Paul all night long."

"I thought you were put out with me," I say. "I felt a distinct chill in the air."

"Since when did that ever stop you from communicating?" he says. "You, of all

271

people — you never met a rebuff you couldn't talk your way through."

"Well, that was when I was dealing with you mano a mano — I'm more intimidated when third parties are involved."

"I don't see you intimidated by your high school friend, but I won't argue with you," he says.

"Oh, come on — argue with me."

"Well, for starters," he says, "you've run off two or three times today when you were supposed to be with me. Why did you think I drove up here?"

"Maybe that's the crux of it, honey," I say. "Two weeks ago I couldn't pay you to come to the banquet — you were saying things like how you hated these events, how you might have to work — anything you could think of as an excuse. Then this murder takes place and all your antennae pop up. So why *did* you drive up here? You already came up Friday during the day."

I swore to myself I wouldn't get into this kind of discussion with him in public — especially with Josie around, not to mention Paul. But he lucks out — just as he's searching for an answer, Essie Sue gets up and clinks her glass — an action that usually brings angst to all who know her.

"Ladies and gentlemen, your rapt attention please."

Paul gives me a quick glance and shakes his head. We're both hoping Kevin's accomplished his mission with Francie by now. I've lost track of the clock because of my *do* with Ed, but I think Kevin's had enough time to tell about the chip if he didn't waste too many words getting to the point. Neither of us dares look their way. I'm also realizing Francie might not be as likely to report to Freddie in the middle of Essie Sue's harangue, whatever it turns out to be.

"I'd like everyone connected with the planning and coordination of this unforgettable reunion to be recognized," Essie Sue says. "So as I point to your table, would all the temple volunteers please stand up for your applause."

"Ruby," Josie says to me across the table, "do I let them take the rabbi's dinner plate away? They're getting ready to serve the dessert soon."

"Just keep it there if you can," I say. "He might want it."

I look around to see if Freddie has displaced Kevin from his seat next to Francie yet. Freddie's just coming back to the table and sitting down, but instead of heading back our way, Kevin is still there. Francie has insisted on having the waiter pull over an extra chair for Kevin, who has that *I-need-help* look he gets whenever his plans don't work out. I see him making excuses to get back and eat his dinner, but Francie's insisting, despite the fact that Freddie's ready to dig into his own meal.

"What the hell is this?"

We can hear Freddie all over the room. He's looking at something on his plate.

"What is it?" Paul says to me.

"Just something extra I thought might disturb him," I whisper. "I bought a plastic egg and tipped the waiter to add it to Freddie's dinner plate — I told him it was a practical joke for Freddie's birthday."

"You shouldn't have done it without telling me," Paul says.

"Okay," I say, "but you have to admit, it's working. You wanted him upset."

"Under the circumstances, it could help, but on principle I don't like it, Ruby."

"He hasn't put it all together yet," I say, "but he will when Francie tells him about the chip."

Which is what she seems to be doing right now as they're talking together, with Kevin struggling to get up from his chair. Francie's holding Kevin's hand in place —

I'm sure she knows Freddie will want to question him.

I can't tell exactly what's going on since Essie Sue's continuing with the program of the evening. She's pointing to our table, so as the only volunteer here, I have to stand.

"Thank you, Ruby Rothman," she says. "Ruby, as you all know, is the widow of our late deceased rabbi, Stu Rothman. I must say, Ruby, and I'm sure everyone will agree, you're more cooperative since your husband passed away than you ever were in the old days. Let's give Ruby a hand."

I acknowledge the backhanded compliment with the savoir faire of all those who can no longer be astonished by anything Essie Sue comes up with. Paul and Ed are another story, however — I'm mentally noting their snickers for later retribution.

"Passing on to even more important supporters," Essie Sue says — managing to zing me once again, "this assembly should observe that the next table is a truly stellar one. My cousin Heather Epstein and her husband Mo have devoted countless hours to overseeing the printing of our menus and program notes. Since Mo, as you all know, is the owner of Eternal's own Pandemonium Printing Company, it is with selfless devotion that he relinquished the job at hand to Kinko's, which was cheaper."

We all clap for Mo, who ain't so dumb. He told me he realized, after only three committee meetings, that separating Essie Sue from his livelihood was a good thing, even if it meant giving the reunion job to his biggest competitor. As he says, "Let the big guys eat the profit — they only had to print the batch over four times."

"Hey, Essie Sue . . ." Bubba Copeland, ever vigilant, waves his hand. "You've covered almost every table. Aren't you giving any credit to your cochairman tonight?"

"Everything in its time, Bubba. There are many essential cogs here besides the leadership — I intend to honor the little people at the wheel."

That didn't come out too well, but it did shut up Bubba. It also unfortunately spotlighted Freddie's table when that's the last thing we needed.

Paul jerks his head around to see what's going on in the cochair's spot, and it's not ideal. Kevin's still trying in vain to get back to our table while Freddie's face is going from red to ashen and back again as he listens to Francie. I'm hoping Kevin's remembering Paul's assurances that he's covered if anything goes wrong. For now, I'm not taking my eyes off him.

"I think the time has finally come to let you all in on my surprise," Essie Sue announces, tapping her glass again. We all know a diversion when we see one, and she's obviously determined not to give public credit to Freddie, no matter what.

"Helpers, on with the show."

She points her hand at one of the Temple Teens up front, who starts a stereo system amplified to ensure deafness within audible range. Then she signals to the headwaiter, who, at the worst possible time, plunges the banquet hall into total darkness.

Paul reaches for my hand in the dark, and I grab hold rather than try to say anything in his ear. I think we're saying plenty — that this whole plan of ours could unravel.

"People, this is way beyond the pièce de résistance — this will be a spectacular display." Essie Sue, successfully outshouting her musical background — a feat in itself — orders the waiters to parade through the hall with trays of flaming desserts held over their heads.

"Forget Alaska," she says. "Give a rousing hand for Baked Burning Bush, in remembrance of our biblical ancestors' first attempts at fire."

She has that wrong as usual, but we have other conflagrations to deal with. The lights are still out, and the crowd is applauding, although not for long.

"It's imitation meringue over vanilla ice milk," she assures us, "just in case you were worried about the calories."

By the time the lights go on so that we can enjoy our just desserts, Paul's let go of my hand and is in deep conversation with Betsy, who's nodding her head.

"What's the matter?" Ed leans over and says to me. "You're not letting Essie Sue get to you, are you?"

"I'm okay, honey, but you'll have to excuse me."

Before I even look over at the other table, I know what I'm going to see. Or not see.

I hate it that my intuitions never fail me at times like this. Sure enough, Freddie's missing from his seat. And so is Kevin.

37

"Now what do we do?" I say to Paul. "And what do I do about Ed?"

"No one's paying attention to the rabbi's meanderings," he says, "so I don't think Ed will notice unless you bolt on him. Let me take care of it — that's what I brought another cop along for. Just mellow out and let me find them — they can't have gone far."

Paul and Betsy excuse themselves and leave the table.

"I guess they have to check in with someone," I say, somewhat pathetically to Ed and Josie. "Just leaves us, I guess."

"She's his date, right?" Ed says. "So what do you mean *they* have to check in with someone?"

"I just meant she's going with him, obviously. She came with him."

"Speaking of dates, where's *my* dinner partner?" Josie says. "What happened to the rabbi?"

"Doing what Essie Sue told him to do," I say. "Unless he escaped for a while."

"No," Josie says. "He told me he wanted to come back to that food — he would have escaped back here, if anywhere."

"Let's get the waiter to clear it," I say. "It looks disgusting now that it's cold. We'll order him something from the hotel café if we have to."

None of us dares touch the imitation dessert that's being placed in front of us. The meringues look like cement.

"How much did this dinner cost?" Josie asks.

"Fifty bucks," Ed says. "We could have had a good steak with extras across the street for that price."

I'm caught between my worry about what Freddie's doing to Kevin and Paul's warning not to alert Ed. My instinct is to race away and help Paul, regardless of how it looks.

"Having a great time, people?" Essie Sue plops down in Paul's seat next to me, as if things weren't frustrating enough. Now I'll arouse her curiosity, too, if I get up from the table.

"We thought we might leave early," Ed says, seconded by an enthusiastic nod from Josie.

That takes me by surprise, but fortunately, Essie Sue's having none of it.

"Not yet," she says. "There's one surprise left."

I'd feel a lot better if I thought that were true — the night's far from over.

"I'll make my announcement from here," she says, clinking on my glass. Maybe she thinks if she's ensconced at our table she can keep us from leaving.

"I know all of you," she says, "are anxious to hear the results of our exclusive reunion poll, and I'm here to report to you."

She takes some papers out of her purse and shushes the crowd.

By the time Essie Sue gets to the third poll result — the answer to: Has this reunion made you feel closer to (a) God, (b) your fellow man, (c) Eternal, (d) Temple Rita, (e) the Jewish people — I can't take it anymore and decide this might be the best time to bolt. Essie Sue's preoccupied and won't be able to run after me, and I'll take my chances with Ed and Josie. Not only do I not care what percentage of our group voted for any of the above, I'm beginning to panic on Kevin's behalf.

"Ladies' room," I say before I run for it, and I make it a point not to look back.

As I pass the swinging doors to the kitchen, I do a double-take.

The top half of the doors are glassed in — to avoid accidents when the waiters go in and out, I suppose. I could swear I saw

Kevin's head pop up in one of the glass panes. I look again and see him beckoning to me with his hand — then he disappears again.

I look around and see that no one in particular is paying attention to me, and then pull one of the doors open as gently as possible in case someone's coming through with a tray.

The kitchen's bustling, and sure enough, two waiters are right in front of me, trying to get out the doors to serve coffee. I stay along the edge of the room and aim for an out-of-the-way corner before trying to make contact with Kevin. Better to let him find me.

"Hey, Ruby — over here," he says.

I motion for him to come to me, and he creeps over in a stooping position. The staff is far too busy to notice us in the corner of the huge kitchen area.

"Stay here," I say. "Is it safe in the kitchen?"

He looks at me as if I were nuts. "What's safe?" he says. "Freddie's after me."

"But he's not in the kitchen, right?"

"Not for now at least."

"Okay," I say, "then I think we should stay here while you catch me up on what's happening. This is a dark corner and everyone's too busy to notice us." I perch on a wooden case of some sort and Kevin squats beside me.

"Are you hurt?" I say.

"No. I got away from him. But he's looking for me."

"Start with when the lights went out. No, start with when you went over to the table and saw Francie. What happened?"

"Well, I made small talk like I hate, said I was visiting each table, and then I mentioned that I wasn't feeling too great. She asked why and I told her I'd been having an attack of the guilts ever since I held something back from Essie Sue. Of course, she was curious to know what that was, and I told her about Essie Sue warning me not to touch the chopped liver mold when I photographed it for her that afternoon of the murder. I told her about biting down on the nut and breaking the tooth, which she knew of course. Then I worked the conversation around to the fact that you'd discovered it wasn't a nutshell or anything like that, but a computer chip, and that you'd put the chip in your computer.

"Did you tell her what was on it?"

"I was about to, when Freddie got back to the table. I had told Paul I was okay with talking to Francie but not Freddie —

he doesn't like me. So I figured Francie knew enough from me to shake up Freddie and I could go. When I tried to, she kept holding my hand until she'd convinced him he needed to talk to me. By that time, he was the one keeping me there."

"You couldn't pull away from her and leave?"

"He told me to stay put, and I was afraid not to. His eyes were bugging out of his head, especially when he saw that plastic egg mixed in with his food."

"Yeah, I heard him ask what the hell that was. I did that."

"Great, Ruby, it was like waving a flag in front of a bull."

Kevin's attempts to whisper in the corner of the kitchen are sounding less and less like whispers. "Hush," I remind him. "I know you're upset, but keep it quiet. So what happened next?"

"Well, Francie filled him in on what I'd said so far, and he wanted to know right away what happened with the chip. He made me tell him you'd printed it out, and I told him I'd seen it."

"That's okay, Kevin, Paul knew you might have to spill everything. It's probably better that you did."

"Anyway, I was starting to tell him about

the computer pictures, and I thought he was going to have a stroke. That's when the lights went out, before I got a chance to tell him we'd showed the chip to the police."

"Yeah, that's the part we didn't plan on," I say. "Who knew Essie Sue was going to showcase the desserts in the dark? I panicked when I realized we couldn't protect you with the lights out — Paul had been keeping an eye on you during the whole conversation with Francie. So did he grab you or what?"

"He did worse than that. When the lights went out, he stuck something above my belt in back that felt like the barrel of a gun, Ruby. He just said 'move' and guided my arm."

"*Oy.*"

I'm sick knowing Freddie has a gun out there, unless he was faking it. But if he is a killer, why am I surprised?

"So the lights are still out?" I say. "And he's taking you where?"

"I don't know where — he didn't get that far. I could see the waiters with their flaming torches or whatever, but we were definitely in darkness ourselves — they were coming out one at a time and didn't make that much light. I decided that it was then or never, and I ran for it, knowing he couldn't see where I was going. I stumbled into the kitchen because it was close — not for any other reason. I thought he might follow me, but I guess he didn't. Now I don't know where he is."

"Paul and his police friend are looking for him. When the lights came on, both of you had disappeared."

"Yeah, but he's still after me, Ruby. And he's probably after you, too, now."

38

No one's near the swinging doors right now, and I'd love to get a look at the tables — not that Freddie would come back in. Then again, he might. There's only Kevin's word he had a gun, and Kevin could easily be seen by the police as confused and mistaken. Right now, there's still nothing tying Freddie to the murder. I'm convinced, though, that he's on the edge, and that could help us if it doesn't kill us first.

"This is what I think we should do, Kevin," I say. "We stand up and get into position with a cover story for why we're in here. Since you're the head of the reunion group so to speak, and I'm helping with the banquet, we've every right to be in here checking on more coffee, or more dessert, or whatever. So if someone discovers us now, we have a right to be in the kitchen, even if they do want us out eventually. I'm going to go look out the door pane and see what's happening, and you stay here. But don't look like you've done something wrong if the kitchen staff sees us."

My brain's churning madly while I have

a few seconds to myself. If Freddie's un-sure about what we've told to the police, that explains why he needs to find us. But surely he'd figure Paul knows, unless he's totally lost it.

I peer out the glass pane, but I don't see Freddie *or* Paul in the dinner crowd.

"No one out there for now," I say to Kevin. "How upset was Freddie? Did he seem focused when he pressed the what-ever into your back?"

"When he told me to move, I thought that was pretty focused, Ruby, but his voice was getting really high-pitched. And earlier, he was wild-eyed when he heard we'd found that chip."

"He's unpredictable, then," I say. "Our best chance is that Paul will find him out there."

"Let's stay here," Kevin says, "and let Paul do the rest of this."

"It's a big kitchen," I say, "but I don't feel safe just waiting for him to show up and find us. I think we should leave."

Before Kevin can balk, I stand up and walk over to a kitchen worker.

"Hey," I say. "Is there another way out of here? I need a smoke."

"I'm with you, lady," he says. "Over there near the back wall there's a hallway we use for storage, and that leads to a back exit to the other reception rooms. The smokers go out that way."

"Is this the ground floor or the first?" I ask. "I never remember."

"It's the ground, but you can take an escalator to the first floor."

Kevin's standing there with a look on his face somewhere between petrified and incredulous.

"You're giving up this safe place?" he says.

"If you want to stay here, do," I say. "But I'm out of here."

"Okay, I'll go with you," he says.

We take the storage hallway to a heavy door, and emerge from the kitchen area to the reception rooms. A big sign directs us to the BUSTIN' BRONCOS ROOM, BLAZING SADDLES ROOM, RODEO ROUSTERS, and other western clichés the hotel management obviously feels will attract convention visitors who're expecting Austin to be an outpost and not a high-tech center.

"I thought you didn't want us to be exposed," Kevin says. "What do you think we are now?"

"We can still duck back through this door if we have to," I say. I steer us to a recessed space for telephones — at least we can peer out from here without being so visible.

I hear a buzz of voices and look out from my phone perch. One of the mystery writers' postconvention workshops has just ended, and people are pouring out of the Bustin' Broncos Room. A table has been set up outside the room, and one of the publishing companies is handing out souvenir T-shirts — lime green with fluorescent yellow lettering saying READ US AND TREMBLE on the back. Perfect.

"Follow me," I tell Kevin.

I run for the table before the shirts are all gone, and take the last extra-large on the table for Kevin, and whatever I can grab for me.

"Quick — put this on," I say.

"Why?"

"Later," I say. I jerk mine over my head and try to do the same for him before he can call too much attention to us.

"I can't get this over my jacket," he says.

"Then take it off, but be quick, Kevin," I say. "We can leave it on the table here and pick it up later."

"No, you'll lose it," he says.

I give him a look he can't refuse and he puts the T-shirt on.

We blend in with the crowd, which

seems to be strolling en masse to the escalators up to the lobby.

We hop on, and just as we get almost to the top, I see Freddie, peering out the door of the men's room on the lobby level. I crouch down and tell Kevin to do the same, and we emerge intact with a whole bunch of lime green T-shirts shielding us.

"Now what?" Kevin almost shouts to me.

"Just follow the crowd," I say. I'm afraid to panic him by letting him know I've spotted Freddie. The truth is I don't have anything remotely resembling a plan at this point.

I realize I've made a big mistake not telling him when he once again shouts at me, only this time even louder.

"Ruby, let's go to the cocktail lounge and look for Paul."

I look over my shoulder and see that Freddie's heard Kevin's unmistakable voice, and is coming our way.

"Freddie's heard us," I warn Kevin, "and he's headed over here."

I put my hand on Kevin's shoulder as I shush any reply. "Let me handle it, Kevin, okay?"

Talk about prescience — Kevin doesn't need to *Read Us and Tremble* — he's doing more shaking on his own than his giveaway T-shirt ever hinted at.

I make sure we're still following the group, although it's my luck that it starts dissipating as people get closer to the bar area.

"Where's Paul?" is all Kevin can muster as the crowd scatters.

I turn again and this time look straight into Freddie's eyes. In case I don't get it from his distorted glance, he puts his hand on his belt to caution us not to run.

In the event I might be assuming he's not totally in charge, he gives us a smile with his lips, not his eyes, and puts his arms around both of us.

"So nice to run into you," he says. "Let's go have a talk."

39

"Let's go to your suite," I say, answering cheery with cheery. "We can have privacy."

"Not on your life," he says. "That's the first place the police will look."

"Why do you care what the police think?" I say.

Kevin, still shaking, looks at me like I've gone over the edge, but Freddie's willing to continue the banter. Both of us know we need to establish a neutral ground or we'll never find out what's in the other's mind. Freddie doesn't know how much I've told or why I might be holding back, and I'm not sure if he's really off-balance enough to think he can get rid of us.

"How about the lobby?" Kevin says.

"Oh, sure — that's a lot better," Freddie says.

As I think about it, I realize that I'd rather not be found by Paul right now, either. I can't believe Freddie would shoot us here, if he even has a gun, and I'm pretty certain I can get more out of him than Paul will at this point.

"Head toward that empty meeting room

over there," he says, pointing to Blazing Saddles. We go in and I sit down immediately at a table nearest the door.

"I'm not moving," I say, "it's this table or nowhere."

I pull Kevin down onto the seat beside me, and Freddie sits close to us at the head of the long conference table. He keeps his hand near his belt and under his jacket. I don't see a gun, but who knows — I'll assume he has one. We're both obviously playing out the bluff for what it's worth.

"Why don't you talk, Ruby?" he says. "I hear you've been busy with a computer chip."

I don't answer right away — I'm deciding how far I want to go. I'd like him to think I haven't told Paul yet, but I doubt he'll buy that. I wish, too, that I could tell him I know he was the man who attacked me at the sleep center, but that's not smart for now, either. No use raising his desperation level.

"Yes, the chip landed in my pocket, actually," I say. "The rabbi wanted me to save whatever it was that broke his tooth and give it to the dentist. The dentist didn't ask for it, and when I found it later, I discovered it was a computer chip the rabbi bit down on. Why would you be interested in it?"

"I'm interested in what you did with it,"

he says. "What was on the chip?"

"A bunch of numbers running together," I say.

"Anything else?"

"Some sort of graphic," I say. "It looked like a goblet of some sort, but I'm not sure because the chip must have been damaged when the rabbi bit down on it." That's an idea I hadn't thought of before — it should make Freddie a bit more secure to assume the chip's defective.

"The resolution was grainy," I say, "and like the numbers, the lines all ran together when I tried to print it out. Maybe it had something to do with Hal's killing the stranger — do you think?"

"I have no idea," he says.

"But Hal's innocent. You said so," Kevin says. My hush-up looks obviously aren't working.

"Well, I certainly hoped so, but his prints *were* on the pestle," I say.

"So that's all this is about?" Freddie says. "Some blurred numbers and a picture of a goblet?"

"That's all so far," I say. "I passed it along to the police over a day ago, so if Paul thought anyone else was involved, he's certainly had plenty of time to make an arrest."

I can see Freddie visibly relaxing, and if he thinks this is all we and the police have, he might not see us as an imminent threat.

"I still don't see why you care about this," I say. "What's it got to do with you? You scared the rabbi out of his wits."

"What do you mean *scared in the past tense?*" Kevin says. "I still am. You told me to move out of the banquet hall, and you threatened me with a gun."

Freddie looks at me. "Where did he get this *mishegoss?*" he says. "I never threatened anyone — he's got a great imagination."

"That's not what you said when I did that family funeral last year — you said my eulogy showed no imagination whatsoever."

"Rabbi, let me speak to Ruby without your interrupting, okay?"

"I told you about my involvement," I say. "All I want to know from you is why you ushered the rabbi out of the banquet hall, and why you made us come into this meeting room with you under the pretext of having a gun."

"Just a little joke," he says. "I was curious about the murder, and since the rabbi said you two were helping the police, I figured you'd give me the latest if I badgered you. No harm in that."

"So we can go now?" Kevin says.

"Maybe," Freddie says.

He thinks he's got it made — he's still in no danger of being exposed.

I'm about to tell Kevin we should leave when I see Paul and Betsy searching the room across from ours. Finally.

"Lieutenant Lundy," I call out. "Are you looking for the rabbi and me? We're fine. Just chatting with Freddie here."

I head toward Paul, who's going for his holster. I hold both hands forward and wave them sideways in a *hold* sign — I don't want him jumping the gun, as it were.

"Wait," I say while Freddie's still seated and can't see my face. "He forced us in here and is waffling about letting us leave — says he never had a weapon."

Paul motions to Betsy to go in the room. "Make conversation," he tells her. "I need a minute to talk to Ruby."

We both know this better be quick.

"I told him the chip was damaged," I say, "and I gave it to you but it hasn't been useful so far. We still don't have him, but he's feeling reassured, and not on guard. I have an idea."

"Your ideas have made the last hour a

nightmare," he says. "I thought you could be dead like Max Cole."

"Get Kevin out of there," I say, "and see if Freddie does have a concealed gun. If so, why don't you let Betsy take him to the station while you and I find Francie? She's got to know about the murder. I don't believe he could have taken the platter up to their hotel suite and then to their house without her seeing it."

"She could panic and talk to us if she thinks her husband's been arrested," Paul says.

"It's worth a try," I say.

Paul steps in the room where Freddie's still seated and giving a good imitation of looking innocent.

"Hello, Lieutenant," he says. "Any progress on the killing? I was just discussing it with the rabbi here and Ruby."

I kick Kevin's foot as discreetly as possible under the circumstances and take him out of the room.

"I'm going to have to search you, Mr. Fenstermeister," Paul says. "I've had a complaint concerning a weapon."

In about two seconds flat, Paul comes up with a small handgun stuck in Freddie's waistband.

"Hey, wait a minute," Freddie says. "I

have a right to carry a gun. Ask Ruby —
she and the rabbi were just leaving — nobody's keeping anybody. I want my
lawyer."

"Take your time," Paul whispers to Betsy
before joining us out in the hallway.

We head for the banquet, where Essie
Sue is undoubtedly still holding the reunion group hostage to her own special
brand of entertainment.

I'm determined not to let Paul know
how glad I am to see him — it would destroy my cool. I can't help touching his
arm, though.

"This is a decent plan so far, Ruby,"
Paul says, "but tell me — what would you
have suggested if we hadn't found a gun on
Freddie?"

"To be honest," I say, "I haven't the
slightest idea."

40

Essie Sue has indeed tied and lassoed the crowd — dozens of listless faces are looking upward, as if for divine rescue. The first person we see tells us that Essie Sue's attempts to force the group to line dance failed miserably — *quelle surprise*. The program has moved on to a recitation of the bios of all the reunion guests — big givers first. While attention is focused on Giver Number Seventeen, Kevin slips into a seat at one of the tables in the back of the room — he's dodging Essie Sue's wrath in the likely event she's noticed he's been missing.

"Hey, Ruby," he stage-whispers.

"Quiet, Kevin — you're supposed to be inconspicuous."

"I just want to know where you and Paul are going with Francie — I've been chased all night, too, you know. The least you can do is tell me what's going on."

"We're going up to her suite if she'll take us," I say. "It's quiet there, and private."

Paul nudges me to hurry up and head for Francie's table. Freddie's seat is of course empty, and I grab it while Paul drags a chair over to Francie's other side.

"Do you know where Freddie is?" she whispers. "He's been gone forever — I sent someone to look for him a half hour ago, but they didn't see him. I've called our room several times, too. He was with the rabbi."

"The rabbi's back," Paul says. "Your husband's okay — I've spoken with him within the last few minutes. But I'd really like to speak with you now. Could we go up to your room? I've asked Ruby to come with us in case you're hesitant to have the meeting alone."

"I don't know," she says. "I think I should wait for Freddie — where did you see him? And why do you want to talk to me? He's the spokesman in the family."

"This is important, Mrs. Fenstermeister," Paul says. "It's a police request."

"I think you should come with us, Francie," I say. "I'll be with you."

We take Francie around the back of the room, and mercifully, Essie Sue misses our exit.

We don't say much in the elevator, and we're lucky there, too, because the three of us are alone on the ride up. The suite has a small seating area, and I plan to sit on the sofa with Francie so Paul can pull up a chair opposite her. I don't think we'll have long before Freddie's lawyer calls, so I whisper to Paul that it might be a good idea to take the phone off the hook. He nods *yes* and I go in the bedroom and put the receiver under a pillow.

When I return, Paul has started the questioning — we won't have this chance again. He's not mentioning where Freddie is for now, and I'm sure Francie thinks her husband is still in the hotel.

"You do realize, Mrs. Fenstermeister, that this concerns you, too — not just your husband. When you spoke to the rabbi tonight, we understand that he told you about a computer chip he found in the liver mold at the scene of the Max Cole murder. Apparently, the rabbi broke a tooth biting down on it. We have information about the chip that's vital to our case. So this isn't just idle chatter — it's crucial to our investigation."

"But Freddie's the one to ask. I told him everything the rabbi told me, and then he went with the rabbi outside the banquet room to talk with him. I haven't seen either of them since."

"Do you know what was on that chip?"

"I don't know anything about it, Lieutenant."

"We do. The chip had detailed photos of a blue Fabergé egg, plus instructions for payment to be made, presumably for the egg, and a Swiss bank account number for a further electronic payment. The police want to understand everything you know about that egg."

"Freddie should . . ."

"You, Mrs. Fenstermeister. I'm asking you."

"I'm waiting for Freddie."

Paul makes his move — nothing else is working.

"Your husband has been arrested," he says. "We need your cooperation to clear your name. If you're involved, you could be criminally liable as well."

Francie jumps up and lights a cigarette with a not-too-steady hand.

"Arrested? Are you crazy? What did he do?"

"Did you know he was carrying a gun?" Paul says.

"Of course not. Freddie doesn't even own a gun. And he certainly wouldn't take one to the reunion banquet. Why are you questioning him at all? He's not a part of any murder."

"He's not just being questioned, Mrs. Fenstermeister. He was taken away in handcuffs. Do you understand that these are serious matters? And once again, do you realize you'll be implicated if you know anything about this and don't cooperate?"

I've tried to keep my mouth shut, but I'm thinking she might listen to me, if only because I'm not the police.

"Francie, we've known each other for a long time. Believe me when I say that this isn't just Freddie's problem — it's yours now, too."

She stops pacing and sits back down, sucking on her cig so hard I'm afraid the smoke's going to come out of her ears.

"Okay," she says, "I'm cooperating. Can we keep this short, and can I see Freddie when this is over?"

"One thing at a time," Paul says.

"What are you accusing him of doing with the egg?" she says.

She's obviously not too upset to try to take control and ask the questions herself, but I notice Paul's going along with her.

"You do collect Fabergé eggs as a couple, don't you?"

"Not for a long time. We lost a couple in a burglary a few years ago. His business hasn't gone so good lately — not that anyone's has. So he's not in the market for new ones. What are you saying?"

I make another try. Even though that computer chip shows nothing criminal on its face, it's the connections that count. Maybe I can say something Paul couldn't say.

"The egg I saw on the computer chip looked exactly like the one I've seen many times at your house, Francie. Could he have had an arrangement to sell it and have the proceeds put in a foreign bank account?"

"No, he'd never sell it. He promised me."

Now she *is* distressed. She's just sitting there shaking her head. And chain-smoking. It's obvious that at least this piece of information is a surprise to her.

"How about the day of the murder?" Paul asks. "You told us your husband was with you. But during that afternoon, did he happen to bring the liver mold back to your suite?"

"I can't talk about anything more," she says, getting up again. "Do I have to answer these questions?"

"You indicated you wanted to cooperate," Paul says.

"Well, I've given you all the information I know. I want you two to leave now so I can see Freddie."

"We'll leave then, Mrs. Fenstermeister," Paul says. "I have to get down to the station."

"I'll take her to see Freddie," I say to Paul. "Can you excuse me for a minute, Francie?"

I walk Paul out.

"Maybe I can get something out of her," I say. "You can see it's not dangerous to leave me with her."

"No, I don't think she's dangerous," he says. "But don't try too long. She might need to think about this, and I don't want you pushing her back to the other side."

"She's already *on* the other side," I say, "although I do think she was surprised by a lot of what you told her."

"She's cooler than she looks, but she's not that good a liar," Paul says. "It's obvious she knew about that liver platter. There's no way he could have taken that back to the suite and then put the clean platter back in his own kitchen without Francie knowing. I mean, it *is* possible, but not probable. Bring her down to see Freddie soon, Ruby — that might spark something."

I go back into the room fast before she decides to use the phone and finds it off the hook in the bedroom. She's smoking and sitting.

"You know, Francie," I say, making the most of my time, "if Freddie brought back the State of Texas mold to your room, and traces of the liver from it were found on Max Cole's face, he's in serious trouble."

"But Hal's fingerprints were on the murder weapon," she says.

"Forget Hal for a minute. You think they can ignore asking why Freddie would grab that mold right under the victim's nose?"

"Sorry, Ruby. You're not getting more from me. I want to see my husband."

Right on cue, as if he'd heard her, a key turns in the lock and the door to the suite opens. I can't believe what I'm seeing. It's Freddie.

41

"What are you doing here, Ruby?"

"What are *you* doing here?"

I'm sorry for blurting that out, because I'm not the police and he has a perfect right to enter his own hotel room. But I'm shocked to see him. I'd planned on noodging Francie, not Freddie, and I'm mustering everything I have to keep my cool.

"You didn't think with my reputation in town that I'd stay at the police station for long on a triviality, did you? Ben Marks had me out on bail in an hour. If you've engineered this just to save your old friend Hal, you've got a lot to answer for."

"I'm an old friend of yours and Francie's, too," I say. That goes over like the feeble retort that it is.

"Oh, a very good friend of ours," he says. "That's why I caught you snooping in my study when you were at our home."

He should only know I questioned his cook, too, but I don't think Beverly passed along the fact that she took time off from her duties to visit with me. I'm also thankful I didn't tell Beverly about finding Essie Sue's silver platter in their kitchen cabinet — at least, I'm hunching it was Essie Sue's.

"Honey, what happened?" Francie says. "What did they want you for? I was so anxious I got another one of those migraines."

"It was nothing, Francie — everything's fine."

"But I want to know what went on at the police station," she says. "Ruby said . . ."

"I don't want you upset about what Ruby says," he tells her. "Let me talk to Ruby. Why don't you go lie down?"

I guess she'll notice the phone off the hook in the bedroom, but I can't worry about it now.

"How long have you been here?" he asks.

"Awhile," I say, "ever since the police left after questioning your wife."

That gets his attention. "Her? What would she know?"

"Oh, they wanted to corroborate her conversation with the rabbi at the table tonight, and some other stuff."

"What other stuff?"

"Don't worry, Freddie, your wife is very loyal — you can ask Lieutenant Lundy. She refused to tell him anything."

"Francie's a trouper," he says, "she

doesn't lose her cool."

I'll bet. She certainly looked nervous when Freddie walked in, and she's always been high-strung. If he's got any sense, he knows she's a loose cannon. If I'd had more time with her, I'd have proven it.

Freddie pours himself a drink from the fancy bar dividing the kitchenette from the living room, and sits down beside me on the sofa. It's a straight-up Jack Daniel's, and I could use maybe a fourth that size myself, but he doesn't offer.

I feel as if I've wasted the interview with Francie by getting nothing out of her, and now I'm about to do the same with Freddie. If his lawyer made bail already, I'm sure he said nothing much to the police. Ben Marks wouldn't have let him do much talking. We need the kind of break that has to come from him, and it's not happening.

"So what were you doing, Ruby — telling Francie a bunch of lies about me?"

"Actually, I was doing more listening than talking."

He gazes at me over the rim of his glass. Not a look of alarm, exactly, and it vanishes instantly to be replaced by a calmer glance, which I notice is sustained with great effort.

Freddie's doing well — in fact, he's done well all night so far, but I'm thinking for the first time I might have a way in.

He's relaxed on the surface as he takes another sip of his drink, and I do likewise with nothing to imbibe. Too bad I don't smoke — this would be a great time to take a long, smooth drag and make him wait.

"You know," I say, "women are never happier than when the men get out of the room and they can let their guard down. As you say, Francie's a trouper, and she handled the police interview very well. When it was over and the door was closed, she was quite relieved."

"So why did *you* stay?"

"So she'd have somebody to talk to."

"Because you're such an old friend."

"Right."

I'm blowing invisible smoke rings just about now.

Freddie's matching me, move by move. He finishes his drink and pours another. Then he turns to the kitchen area, brings out a big block of Cheddar from the refrigerator, and puts it on a wooden tray.

"Want some?" he says.

"Sure."

I slice myself a piece — no crackers offered, and I'm not pushing.

I wait and he waits, and finally he goes on.

"So what did Francie say?"

I can tell he thinks this came out too fast, so he backtracks. "I mean, were you able to calm her down after the police left?"

"She was pretty calm all along," I say.

"So what did she say to you? If she'd had anything interesting to report, I'm sure she would have told the police."

"Well, you can always double-check with her," I say, "but I doubt she'd tell you if anything slipped out in our conversation, do you?"

He doesn't answer, but that's one for my side. I'm being totally forthright about wanting him to check with Francie, and at the same time I'm confirming what he already must know about her.

"So what did she say to you?"

I wonder if he realizes he's asked that same question three times now. Not cool.

"You mean what did we talk about?"

I guess he does realize he's pushing, because he retreats and accepts my more oblique question.

"Okay, what did you talk about?"

"Well, we had a whole discussion about exactly what happened in the late after-

312

noon on the day of the murder. You know — the day you and Francie were in the suite here together."

I start to go on, and then decide to switch subjects before he can ask me again what she told me. If I'm right, there's so much he wants to keep from me that he'll want to hear whatever I bring up at this point.

He's put his drink down *and* his cheese.

"We also talked about your fabulous Fabergé egg collection," I say, "and about how some of them were stolen in that burglary you had a while back. I understand you were never going to sell the blue egg Francie loved so much. Or at least, not without telling her."

I want to feed him something I know for sure, and since I don't exactly have a trove of information to draw from, I'm being stingy and hoping what I give him will work. No use concentrating on the computer chip yet, either — we've discussed that, if you can call answering under gunpoint a discussion. Hopefully, he still thinks the graphic and text were blurry, and that the egg looked like a goblet on the printout. And as long as I can avoid his talking to Francie right now, he won't find out what she already knows — that the

313

graphic clearly shows the egg and the bank account numbers.

But what can also get him into trouble is anything Francie might have said to me. His wife might not be required to testify at trial, but I'm sure that's the last thing he envisions — he's not planning on getting anywhere near a courtroom. So far, he's avoided having any evidence stick to him, but that could change if Francie's given up anything important. Which she hasn't, of course.

"Why are you so interested in our Fabergé collection?" he asks.

"Just something that happened to come up when she was talking about the hard luck with money you've had lately — not that everyone else hasn't had problems, too. She wanted me to know you'd never sell the blue egg."

"That's our business, though — right? What we do with our possessions?"

"Sure. Francie just seemed a little upset in general, what with the murder and all the chaos around that. And then there was your bringing the liver mold up to the suite . . ."

"She said *what?* She'd never —"

"Never tell on you? If she were afraid of being incriminated herself, she might have," I say.

"Forget incrimination," Freddie says. "You just told me the lieutenant got nothing out of her."

"That doesn't mean she didn't confide in me," I say.

"But nobody else knows, right?"

I'm a moment late in realizing I've gone a teeny bit too far in making Freddie nervous. My job was to get Francie to confide in me, not Freddie — Paul doesn't even know he's loose yet. Which is exactly the problem.

We stare at one another. It doesn't take brains to know there's a small window of opportunity here, and it's not mine.

42

I jump for the door at the same time Freddie jumps for the cheese knife, and he's faster. He grabs me around the neck from behind and waves the cutting edge in front of me.

"It's sharp *enough*," he says in answer to my unasked question. "Messier than a finer blade would be, but it'll do the job. I wouldn't struggle too much if I were you — I could stumble and have an unfortunate accident. In fact, that's exactly what's going to happen, Ruby — you're going to have an unfortunate accident. This penthouse has a door leading right to the roof."

I scream and Francie comes running into the living room. She's groggy.

"I took a pill and dozed.

"My God, Freddie — let her go," she yells as she gets her bearings — "you're no killer."

My mind's racing. She sounds too sincere to be faking — there's nothing like crisis — or waking from sleep — to bring out the truth, and I can tell Francie doesn't know he killed Max. He must have told her some other story as to why he was getting rid of the liver mold that afternoon, and she's helping him cover it up. If she's not in on the murder, maybe she'll help me.

"Who are you to tell me not to save myself?" he says. "You got me into this."

Freddie's enraged, but it's directed toward Francie at the moment. Not that he's made any effort to move the crook of his arm from my windpipe. I'm more afraid of choking to death than I am of the cheese slicer, although I guess it's a toss-up.

"What do you mean?" she yells at him. "I didn't tell Ruby a thing."

"Sure," he says, "I know all about it."

Okay, this is my chance. If I let her convince him she kept her silence, she'll have no reason to help me. I start gurgling and swaying — I'm not too good at it, but it works.

"Release her throat, Freddie — she's about to faint. Do it. Ruby, promise you won't scream."

I guess she still wields some influence, because he does it. I nod that I won't yell, and he holds me tight, but lets me breathe again without wheezing. I'm not sure I can talk, but it's not as if I had a choice — I've got to get Francie on my side.

"Francie, look at us here," I say. "If he

kills me, you're an accomplice. The police know about Freddie — you've got to save yourself. And maybe you can help him, too."

"What have you gotten yourself into?" she says.

"You bitch — you spilled your guts to Ruby. We *have* to get rid of her."

I interrupt before she can contradict him. "Freddie, the police know about that afternoon, and they know more about what's on the computer chip than you think. Tell him what was printed out, Francie — make him think about what he's doing."

"They know about the Fabergé egg, Freddie," Francie says. "They have the bank account numbers and color photos of our blue egg. The one you promised me you'd never sell."

Better than I thought, even. She's assuming it's their egg, even though at the moment there's no exact identification. He'll believe we have more than we *have* on him, to put it crudely.

"They got to you, didn't they?" he says.

Again I push myself in ahead of Francie. If I try to speak for her, maybe she'll forget about answering.

"Francie loves you, Freddie. She doesn't

want to see you destroy yourself, or her."

"It's no good, honey," Francie says. "We've got good lawyers for the rest, but you'll never get away with killing Ruby. You know that."

"I don't know any such thing," he says, pulling me toward a door in the hallway. "I'm thinking she's the only one you've told the whole story to — even Ruby said you didn't tell the police."

"I didn't tell anything to Ruby or the police," Francie says. "You're safe. And I'll say it again — you're not a killer yet."

"If he's not a killer yet," I say, "then what is he protecting by getting rid of me? Why would he risk it over some crooked dealings his lawyers can handle? I'm telling you, Francie, he murdered Max Cole."

"Which is why you should think twice about opening your mouth to anyone else, Francie," Freddie says. "Once we take care of Ruby, we're safe."

Finally that got her attention — she reacts to Freddie with a look that makes slack jaw seem trifling — she's literally stultified with disbelief.

"Run, Francie," I say. "Get help."

"She won't go," Freddie says. He opens the door to the roof and shoves me ahead of him. I can feel the knife on my neck. I'm still counting on Francie, though — nobody could be that loyal, or stupid, or both.

"Follow us, Francie," he says from the stairs. "It'll all be over in a minute and you and I will take that nice, long cruise I promised you. Do anything else and your whole life will change."

To my amazement, she's right behind us on the steps. I stumble and she actually helps Freddie push me the rest of the way. So much for the truth setting me free.

The roof is a sunning area. No one's here at night — just my luck there's not a lovers' tryst to interrupt. Freddie's arm is blocking my windpipe again — a smart move on his part, since if I'm going to die anyway I certainly don't have to go silently. We sashay over to the waist-high ledge, and I try kicking him away. I took two karate lessons once, but apparently that's not enough.

"Grab her ankles," Freddie says.

Francie catches one of my feet in mid-air and holds on to it.

We hear banging noises down the stairs.

"You didn't close the damn door to the roof?" Freddie whispers.

I still can't say anything. If Francie weren't here helping him, I know I could either break away momentarily or yell — one or the other. But with two of them on me, I'm stymied. And terrified.

It's got to be Paul and the police — either that or the hotel security people. No one else would knock on the suite door that loudly. Paul's had just enough time to drive to the station, look for Freddie in one of the interrogation rooms, and find him gone. Maybe he called for help until he could get back here.

"Now what?" Francie says, still holding my leg.

"We hurry, that's what," Freddie says. "See what you got us into?"

"Fred Fenstermeister, listen to me. I did not say one word to Ruby. Understand?"

Francie jams up against him to emphasize her point. I use the few seconds when they're more interested in who's right than in me to make my move. I break free for the brief moment Freddie's distracted and yell.

"Up here! On the roof."

They both grab me again, but this time, we struggle. And the longer we can scuffle, the more time the posse'll have to break down the door to the suite. Since I'm trying to avoid getting cut as well as being thrown over the ledge, though, my options are limited.

"Come on," Freddie tells Francie. "Get her over the edge. We can say she lost her balance and we tried to save her."

They try to gather me up again, rather successfully, but Freddie can't quite maneuver me around to resume his choke hold. I'm yelling *murder* this time — if they're going to do it, I'll be damned if they get away with calling it an accident.

Through all our racket I hear a voice saying, "Stop. It's over. Hold it."

A head pops up from the stairs. It's Betsy, Paul's undercover date, with her gun pointed at us. She must have been the first to see that Freddie's bail was posted and he was free to go.

"You're surrounded," she says. "Paul's on his way," she says to me.

Freddie drags me the last few inches and leans me over the low railing, but I can't help noticing that Francie drops my leg like it was one of Milt's hot bagels.

"Come any closer and she's on the roof of the Sharper Image," Freddie says, his head indicating which direction I'd have to fall to get there from the hotel roof.

Two more policemen flank Betsy now, but Freddie's panicking. He has me backward and shoves my head over the rail.

"If you want her alive, you'll back off," he says.

"Give it up, Fenstermeister." It's Paul's voice, and even though I have no reason to be relieved yet, I am.

Freddie stops short, which is a good thing, except that the abrupt movement causes the cheese knife to penetrate my upper arm like — well, cheese.

Don't ever let anyone tell you that in the midst of shock you don't feel anything until later.

I start gushing blood like a lawn sprinkler, and the sight of it seems to paralyze Freddie. He drops the knife and loosens his grip on me, too, for a minute. With my mind on the cut, I can't take advantage of the distraction to twist away. He eases me to the edge of the balustrade just as Paul jumps him.

He pushes Freddie aside and throws me over his shoulder like a baby — fortunately gently like a baby, too.

Francie's just standing there staring at Freddie. "Now look what you've done," she tells him.

"What *we've* done," Freddie says, "don't forget that."

"Handle them," Paul says to Betsy and the other cops, and then strips off his shirt and makes a tourniquet of it. He's good at it — the bleeding slows to a trickle.

He picks me up again — still gingerly I'm glad to say, since my whole side's killing me — and takes me down the stairs to the suite. He lays me on the couch and sits down, too, so that my head is cradled in the crook of his elbow. His free hand is supporting my bad arm, keeping it from dangling off the sofa.

"They've already called for help," he tells me. "My favorite EMS crew — they'll get here faster than a speeding bullet, Wonder Woman."

"You're not going to bawl me out for provoking them?"

"I never yell at my favorite people while they're bleeding," he says.

"How come your eyes are red?" I say.

"I was scared."

"When did *that* start?" I ask him.

"Give it a rest, Ruby. Nobody hurting like you must be should be so observant, anyway. Why aren't you moaning and groaning like a normal person?"

"I thought sure she'd turn on him," I say, changing the subject since he's already dodged it.

"When I got back to the station and found out Fenstermeister was gone, I knew he'd head straight back to the hotel to make sure of Francie's silence. My stomach felt like it had dropped to my shoes."

"Yeah, he didn't exactly expect me to be here," I say.

"If I'd been here, I wouldn't have let you start in on him," Paul says.

"And if you'd been here, he'd still be free on a minor weapons charge," I say.

"You don't get it, do you, Ruby?"

"Get what?" At this close range, I can smell his aftershave, his sweat, the leather from his shoulder holster, and his hair, which gets curly when he needs a haircut.

"It's not worth it. A collar's not worth it, solving the murder's not worth it — nothing's worth it."

"Me?"

"Yeah, you. Who else is sitting here?"

43

"I'm so glad to see you all on this wonderful Monday morning in our beloved Eternal. I know all of you will long remember this reunion," Essie Sue says after tapping her glass to bring today's farewell brunch to order.

"*Memorable*'s not the word, Essie Sue," Bubba Copeland says. "I'm trying to forget as much of it as possible."

Bubba gets many clinks in response.

"Don't be a spoilsport, Bubba — you always were a downer."

"No, I'm just a well-balanced guy," he says, "as opposed to unbalanced."

"Let's forget Bubba — and give a big hand to my wonderful committee for bringing us to this day. Rabbi, can you give us a blessing?"

"You didn't tell me I had to participate this morning," Kevin stage-whispers to Essie Sue. He's seated next to her on the makeshift podium Milt's set up facing the other tables at The Hot Bagel.

"I shouldn't have to tell you — it's your job," she whispers back. "And don't tell me you can't pull an invocation out of your repertoire."

"What repertoire?" he says to me. I'm sitting on his other side, or rather, leaning in my weakened state. My arm's bandaged all the way to the shoulder.

"Why don't you just talk to them?" I say. "Tell them what you're thankful for this morning. She's feeling emotional, and after this week, who can blame her?"

He's on his feet at least.

"I'll just say a few words," he says. "We should be very thankful today that Hal Margolis is out of the hospital and out of suspicion."

That could have been put a bit more delicately, but it's a start, and it makes Essie Sue dab her eyes, which is also good for Kevin.

"I'm glad Ruby Rothman's arm isn't broken — only slashed, and that the police caught Max Cole's killer during our Sunday night banquet. I mean, I'm not glad, exactly, since it's our Founding Nephew who's being charged, so we're all sorry about that, not glad."

He leans over to my ear. "Are we glad, or sorry, Ruby? I mean, he *is* a killer. I get mixed up when I'm winging it."

"I'd just leave it at that," I say. "Wind it

327

up. I don't want to sit here any longer than I have to."

"In closing, I guess reunions can bring together a bunch of odd fellows," he says. "I mean odd women and fellows.

"Is that nonsexist enough?" he whispers again. "I didn't mean to get into *that* can of worms. Not worms, either, Ruby — you know what I mean."

"Yeah, I do, but let's don't push our luck, Kevin. Wrap it up."

"Well, thank you, Lord. Amen."

He can't miss noticing that he's being glared at by several women.

"Uh-oh," he says. "Strike the *Lord.*"

He's about to explain that, but with my good arm, I pull him down in his seat.

I signal to Milt, who's been pacing back and forth in the kitchen, and the extra wait staff we've hired files into the room with platters of steaming bagels, lox, and other goodies. No chopped liver, though — under my strict orders. The reunion guests breathe a collective sigh that the program is at least temporarily suspended.

"I wasn't ready for the food to be served, Ruby," Essie Sue says.

"Well, Milt was," I say. "We have scrambled eggs on the menu, and we don't want them cold.

"Essie Sue," I say, "why don't you just let people talk and eat for the rest of the brunch? I don't think they need more formalities — let's relax. Go mix with the crowd if you're still feeling hostessy."

The room's buzzing, and I think she actually gets my point. At any rate, she stops emceeing and samples a few calories — very few.

Milt signals me from the kitchen, and I see Paul's tousled head pop up. At the same time, Essie Sue takes up my suggestion to table-hop. Goody — her timing's perfect.

I put my cream-cheesed pumpernickel bagel on a napkin and take it with me to the kitchen, where Paul's waiting for me. We give each other the kind of quick hug and kiss friends do when they've shared something difficult. So I don't get it when Milt puts his hands on his hips and gives me one of his looks.

"Let's go to my office," I say to Paul. "How about bringing two mugs of Kenya, since half my carrying apparatus is useless?"

"She takes it black," Milt says.

"I know that," Paul answers.

My so-called office is a protuberance off the storage room, but it's mine and I've got

329

it curtained so that it's private.

"How's the arm?" Paul asks as we spread our breakfast goodies on my desk. "You shouldn't be out and about today."

"I know," I say, "but here I am."

He gives me a stare that's a lot like the one I just got from Milt, so I ignore it.

"You've got news?" I say. "The whole place here is already humming with gossip, but nothing more substantive than that Hal is out and Freddie is in — which is pretty much the bottom line, I guess. But I was hoping you could fill me in on the good parts."

"Only for *your* ears right now," he says, "but I owe you that much since you've been smack in the middle of all this. Try not to interrupt too much, okay? I have to get back to the station."

"I'll try. Shoot."

"Well, as you could probably tell last night when Francie dropped your legs like hot coals, she wasn't too far away from deciding to save her own ass. That only intensified when we took her in. She spilled everything she knew. Freddie didn't, but when he and his lawyer saw what she'd said, plus when we confronted them with other stuff we'd dug up, we were well on our way to a plea bargain."

"What was Max Cole's role in all this?"

"You promised, Ruby."

"Sorry — tell it your way."

"Maybe I should try to tell it chronologically," he says, "so here goes.

"It was the usual bogeyman — money. The Fenstermeisters had less and less of it, but they needed more. Their small Fabergé egg collection was real, even though they were well aware most people thought the eggs were replicas."

"Where did the eggs come from?"

"The first Fenstermeister had an ancestor who was a jeweler at the court in St. Petersburg. He and another artisan devised a scam — they made a few counterfeits and substituted them for the real thing. Since there was such a large collection, the fake eggs were never detected. When the family came to America, they smuggled the eggs in with them, but were afraid to touch them for years. Freddie's uncle sold the first one to finance his hat factory — and who knows, maybe that money eventually backed Temple Rita.

"Two or three were secretly passed down to Freddie, who couldn't resist displaying them. His debts, though, were more ominous than his family's — they were gambling debts, not to mention his high living

331

costs. When he started owing the high stakes players, he was *'encouraged'* to make an arrangement whereby he sold off the last egg — the blue one. The egg was to be deposited in a Swiss vault during one of their frequent visits to Europe. Max Cole, a low-level guy in the syndicate, was the go-between. His job was to pick up the computer chip containing the instructions on how to retrieve the egg and the documentation of its authenticity. In return, he was to give Freddie a one-time-only cash payment as a show of goodwill. Other payments would be deposited in a Swiss account after the egg was placed in the bank vault.

"Freddie thought the reunion would be the perfect forum — lots of people who were bringing spouses and other family whom no one had met. He would put the chip in Essie Sue's liver mold for Max to pick up before the reception. If someone were around, they'd simply think Max was sampling the refreshments. There would be no way to connect Freddie and Max."

"Ha," I say. "If the gamblers had known Essie Sue was at the controls, they'd never have used the reunion."

"Turns out that not only did they use it, they thrived on it. And Freddie was almost able to ruin Hal, too."

"But why couldn't Freddie just slip the computer chip to Max at one of the parties?" I say. "Why the elaborate prelude to the meeting at the rest stop?"

"A real pro would have made it simpler," Paul says. "But Freddie was paranoid about being connected to Max Cole in any way — he wanted this initial exchange to be totally anonymous. He didn't even want Max to be able to identify him, and he'd been told Max was simply a functionary who would follow directions explicitly. Freddie felt additionally secure because he would receive the cash advance from the syndicate before he deposited the egg in the Swiss vault.

"My guess is," Paul says, "that the egg was of such value that the buyers were willing to risk the advance to assure Freddie's cooperation."

Paul brings a pot of coffee as well as our mugs — it helps me forget how much I'm hurting. Not that what I'm hearing isn't the best narcotic of all.

"Freddie wore rubber gloves to place the chip in the liver, so that there'd be no fingerprints on it. The plan was to place the chip right at the star in Essie Sue's Texas mold — where she always marked a special place for Eternal, just below Austin. All Max had to do was to look under the star. Freddie didn't want to leave anything to chance, and he couldn't resist sticking around when Max came to dig out the chip. But by then, the rabbi had already been there, and he'd done his own sampling. There was no chip for Max to find.

"Freddie realized he'd have to abandon his attempt at anonymity. He ran over to help Max, who obviously, wasn't too thrilled. He thought he was being double-crossed and that Freddie had made a deal with someone else. When they'd finally messed up the whole mold, Max, infuriated, drew a knife on Freddie and demanded he take him to where the chip was being kept. Freddie knew there was nowhere to go — the chip was gone. He panicked. Freddie grabbed the Margolises' antique brass pestle — part of the display showing how the liver was chopped. He hit and killed Max, and Max dropped forward, his head falling into the mold. Freddie lifted Max's head from the mold, pulled the mold out from the ice tray beneath it, and let Max's face fall into the ice. He pushed the platter back far enough so that Max's upper torso was supported by the table.

"Freddie took the liver mold and the knife back to his suite, using the service elevator. Francie was there and helped him put the liver down the disposal and wash Essie Sue's silver platter, which they later stacked in their kitchen cabinet under a bunch of their own fancier platters."

"So the pestle had only Hal's fingerprints because Freddie was wearing rubber gloves?"

"Yep. I don't think Fenstermeister knew or cared whose fingerprints were on it — he only knew they wouldn't be his. And at the time he hit Max, he probably wasn't even thinking that far ahead — he just didn't want to be knifed. Fenstermeister, I'm sure, thought he and Francie would find the chip somewhere in the mold, but of course they never did — the chip was on its way to the dentist with you and the rabbi. Must have been messy, sifting through the mold before they put it down the disposal."

"What a story," I say. "I just remembered, you promised me that Ed could have a scoop on this. Have you contacted him?"

"Yeah, didn't he tell you? My sergeant left a message on his answering machine in San Antonio — I know he got it because he left me a reply at the station — wants me to call him. I just haven't had a chance."

"I haven't heard from him," I say. "I guess he's not too happy that I left the table last night and never came back. But when Freddie used that gun to usher Kevin and me into that reception room, there wasn't much catching up I could do with Ed. Things happened too fast — before I knew it, I was up at Francie's suite with you. And besides, Ed and Josie seemed ready to take off when Essie Sue's reunion speeches started."

"I'm sure he doesn't know you got hurt," Paul says. "Still, I'd have checked in with you if I'd been in Ed's place."

"No, it was probably my place to keep him clued in," I say. "He was supposed to be my date."

"Ruby, you're telling me that getting knifed and almost being thrown from the roof of the hotel isn't enough of an excuse? Why didn't he follow up when you failed to come back to the table?"

"He thought I took off on another wild chase, I suppose. Which I did."

"But that's you — that's who you are. You weren't deliberately trying to desert him. Wouldn't he have wanted to know you were all right?"

"Did Freddie ever say why he attacked me at the sleep center?" I ask.

"I know when you're distracting me," Paul says. "I guess what's between you and Ed is none of my business, Ruby. But in answer to your question, we told Freddie we now had reason to do a lab test of his skin and blood samples, to see if he were the attacker. He admitted it — said he wanted you off the trail after he caught you in his study, and he just intended to scare you."

"Freddie should have known that would only egg me on, you'll pardon the expression."

"Maybe he doesn't know you as well as I do," Paul says, putting his hand on top of my good one.

"Paul, are you holding my hand or trying to stop me from beating you to that last bagel?"

"That's up to you," he says.

Recipes

Essie Sue's Eternally Good Chopped Liver

1½ pounds chicken livers
½ cup chicken fat, rendered
1 extra-large onion, chopped
3 hard-boiled eggs
½ teaspoon salt
Pinch of black pepper

Broil the livers until cooked through — not rare. Melt the chicken fat in a frying pan together with the chopped onion and cook until brown. Add the chicken livers to the pan and sauté for 5 minutes more.

Use a blender (or processor) to chop the onion, eggs, livers, and seasoning until thoroughly mixed. No need to grind to a paste — consistency as preferred. Refrigerate until served in the shape of your choice.

If you want to work harder, do the chopping on tougher liver with a mortar and pestle like my grandmother did.

(Serves 5)

Essie Sue's Chopped Liver for Unclogged Arteries

3 chicken livers
Pam spray
1 pound firm tofu
1 onion, chopped
3 hard-boiled egg whites
Dash of pepper

Thoroughly broil the chicken livers. Spray the pan with no-calorie Pam. Cook together the livers, small squares of the tofu, and the onion until browned. Blend in a food processor or blender along with the egg whites and pepper.

This recipe works better with guests who have never tasted Jewish chopped liver. Spread on diet crackers.

Serves quite a few . . . people usually only eat one.

Acknowledgments

To my beloved family and dear friends: Suzy Weizenbaum, David Weizenbaum, Jon Weizenbaum and Nancy Nussbaum, Emma and Camille Weizenbaum, Sue and Ned Bloomfield, Lindsy Van Gelder, Kathi Stein, Ruthe Winegarten. To good times this year with my special Birmingham buddies: Carole Simpson, Sandra Sokol, Ruth Fromstein, Ferne Seigel, Anne Silberman, Sandra Russell, and Ramsay High class-mates.

To the Shoal Creek Writers: Nancy Bell, Judith Austin Mills, Linda Foss, Eileen Joyce, Dena Garcia, Karen Casey Fitzjerrell — for helping each step of the way with caring and love.

My thanks always to Susanne Kirk, vice president and senior editor of Scribner, and Helen Rees of the Helen Rees Agency, for their invaluable help, enthusiasm, and support with the Ruby series, and for their personal friendship for so many years. My appreciation to Sarah Knight, Angella Baker, and Cristine LeVasser of Scribner and Joan Mazmanian of the Helen Rees

Agency, and all those at Scribner who helped guide the book along its way.

My appreciation to Charlene Crilley for Ruby's Web site, www.sharonkahn.com.

About the Author

Sharon Kahn has worked as an arbitrator, attorney, and freelance writer. She is a graduate of Vassar College and the University of Arizona Law School. The mother of three, and the former wife of a rabbi, she lives in Austin, Texas. *Fax Me a Bagel*, a Ruby the Rabbi's Wife novel and her mystery debut, appeared in 1998 and was nominated for an Agatha Award. Visit her Web site at www.sharonkahn.com.

The employees of Thorndike Press hope you have enjoyed this Large Print book. All our Thorndike and Wheeler Large Print titles are designed for easy reading, and all our books are made to last. Other Thorndike Press Large Print books are available at your library, through selected bookstores, or directly from us.

For information about titles, please call:

(800) 223-1244

or visit our Web site at:

www.gale.com/thorndike
www.gale.com/wheeler

To share your comments, please write:

Publisher
Thorndike Press
295 Kennedy Memorial Drive
Waterville, ME   04901